NEW HAVEN FREE PUBLIC LIBRA
3 5000 01800 0637
P9-ARF-387

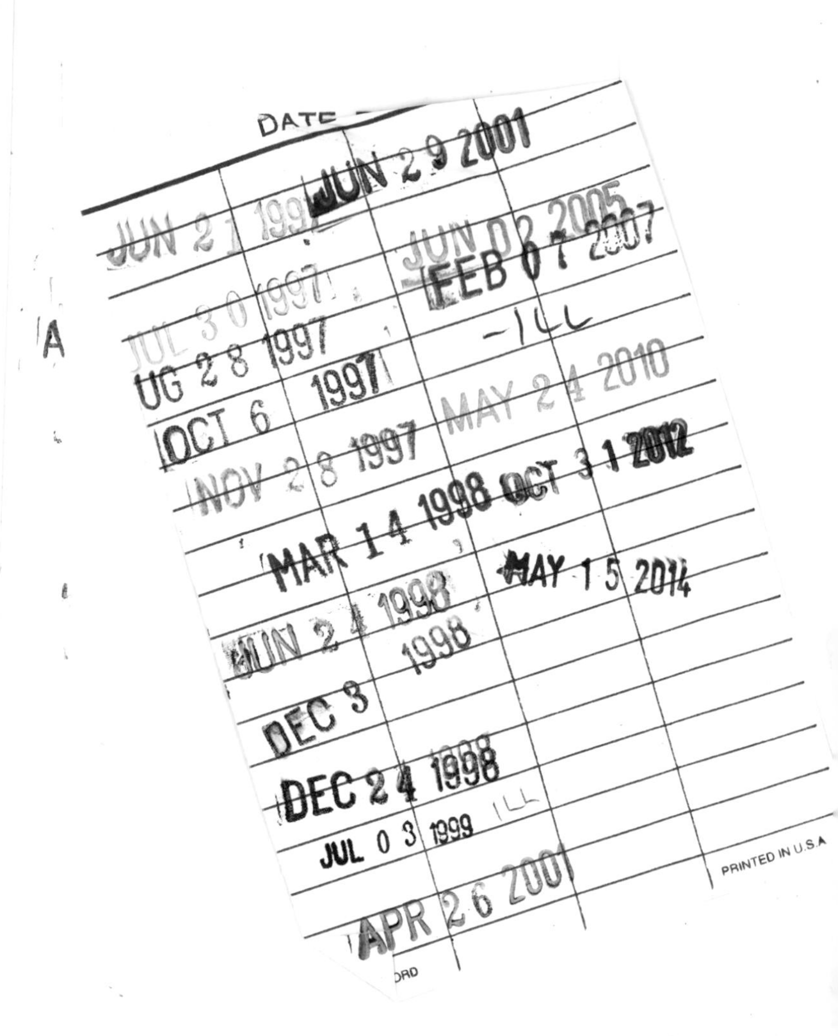
DATE
JUN 2 9 2001
JUN 2 1 1997
JUN 0 3 2005
FEB 0 7 2007
JUL 3 0 1997
-ILL
UG 2 8 1997
OCT 6 1997
MAY 2 4 2010
NOV 2 8 1997
MAR 1 4 1998
OCT 3 1 2012
MAY 1 5 2014
JUN 2 4 1998
DEC 3 1998
DEC 2 4 1998
JUL 0 3 1999
ILL
APR 2 6 2001
PRINTED IN U.S.A.

Mohamed Choukri

STREETWISE

Translated from the Arabic by
Ed Emery

Saqi Books

In-house editor: Jana Gough

British Library Cataloguing-in-Publication Data
A catalogue record for this book is available from the British Library

ISBN 0 86356 093 8 (hb)
ISBN 0 86356 045 8 (pbk)

This edition first published 1996
Saqi Books
26 Westbourne Grove
London W2 5RH

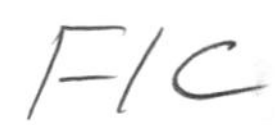

Contents

Contents

Glossary

carajol	coffee with cognac
djellaba	a long, hooded garnment worn by men and women
kif	a type of *hashish* found in North Africa
majoun	a paste made of *hashish*
sabi	the stem of the *kif* pipe, which may be of wood or metal
shaqfa	the clay bowl of the *kif* pipe
taifor	a very low, round table

1

A Flower with No Scent

As I got off the bus I was accosted by a dirty, barefoot kid who couldn't have been more than 10 years old.

'Looking for a hotel, mister?'

'Souq el Kubaybat? Where can I find Souq el Kubaybat?'

'Follow me.'

He looked me up and down and then, glancing at my shabby suitcase, offered to carry it for me. I said no thanks, but I gave him 5 Spanish centimes anyway and he went off happily. The market was packed. There were all the usual food shops, and stalls selling clothing, both new and secondhand. Some people strolled about in the marketplace, while others just sat and watched in the early evening sun. I could hear the sound of Arabic-language radios coming from some of the shops.

After wandering round the market for a while, I asked one of the secondhand clothes sellers where I could find Mr Abdullah's café. He gestured vaguely across the market, and then ambled off shouting his wares to all and sundry.

To the left of the café door stood a wooden counter with *falafel*, fried fish, boiled eggs and a stack of black bread laid out on it, all swarming with flies. Indoors, next to the stove, was a long table with men sitting round it, playing cards. Others were sitting round smaller tables, and most of them were smoking *kif*. It was obvious from their faces and their clothes that they were poor.

A few of them registered my arrival. I sat at a small, dirty table over in one corner and ordered a mint tea from the man at the counter—I presumed he was Mr Abdullah. The *kif* was being sold by an elderly man sitting next to me, who reminded me of Afiouna in Mr Moh's café in Tangier. I bought some. He provided me with a *shaqfa* from his pouch. Whenever I asked him for a *sabi*, he passed me the *shaqfa*, filled with *kif*. I would then pass it back and he either drew on it or handed it on to one of the men sitting next to him.

When Mr Abdullah brought the tea, I asked if he knew the whereabouts of Miloudi, a friend of Hassan el Zailachi.

'I haven't seen him for at least three days.'

As the evening wore on, homesickness and the combined effects of the *kif* and my hunger began to get the better of me. I chatted with the men in the café. We shared our teas, passing them around. I felt comfortable with them. I told them about life in Tetuan and Tangier and they told me what was going on in Larache. One of them said:

'It's like they say: people cry because they've never seen Tangier—but once you've seen it, then you'll cry too.'

The others chimed in:

'A city with a history like that would win anyone's heart.'

'The trouble is, the city's grown ugly, with all the prostitution.'

'Yes, but there's still a lot that's beautiful. And a lot of ancient history too.'

I mooched around in the doorway, wondering how to get something to eat. Even nowadays, every time I find myself ordering a meal in a café I remember those flies around the door as I went in. Mind you, under normal circumstances there's no food I'd turn my nose up at.

I was getting fed up with sitting there and looking at all those stupefied, depressing faces. I was also having difficulty keeping my eyes open. By now most people had left the café, and the chairs and tables were floating before my eyes in a kind of haze. I noticed that there were three rooms leading off from the café. Two of them were locked, but poor-looking people were coming in and out of the third one. As far as I could see, it had bamboo matting on the floor for people to sleep on. I toyed with the idea of asking Mr

Abdullah about the price of a bed for the night there, but I knew that I couldn't afford it. I needed to hang onto my money—I had no idea what this town might have in store for me.

As I sat there half asleep, Mr Abdullah tapped me on the shoulder.

'We're locking up now.'

There were still three men smoking *kif* around one of the card tables. I asked Mr Abdullah if I could leave my bag with him till the following day. He said it would be alright, but he wanted to check what was in it, so I had to show him—two largesh framed pictures, a pair of trousers, two shirts and a pair of socks.

I wandered around the backstreets of the town. No sign of night watchmen or shop security guards. No cars either. Not like Tangier. By this time it must have been well past midnight. I carried on walking for a bit. A town like this wasn't the sort of place to scare you.

It was a mild, moonlit night. I strolled along the promenade overlooking the sea. The night lights were sparkling on the waves. I thought about the nightlife in Tangier, and the way the city lures you to the very edge of death. I thought of the sea-fishing. Places flashed into my mind's eye: Ra's el Manar, Mala Bata, the Caves of Hercules, Sidi Qanqush, El Marisa, El Ramel Qal.

There I was, completely on my own. The moon kept vanishing behind clouds and then reappearing. As I walked through the municipal park I bent down to pick a beautiful white flower, but it had no smell. A forlorn beauty. A flower with no scent. That was probably why nobody had picked it already and it had been left there to grow. In the end, it would either wither and die or be trodden underfoot. On that particular night, I felt I had nothing to lose. I was like that flower, I thought, as I crushed it between my fingers. I could sleep there, or anywhere at all.

The breeze coming off the sea woke me up a bit. I returned to Kubaybat and sought shelter under one of the arches around the square. I squatted against a wall, folded my arms across my knees and rested my head on them. There was no sign of anyone around, no sound of footsteps or anything like that. I don't remember having any thoughts at all. My mind was a blank, as if it had been washed out. Even when I thought about my favourite music, the tunes came into my head and then just disappeared. I had a slight headache, and a throbbing in my brain. It was as if I could hear the beating of my own heart. This was probably the effect of the hunger in my guts and the fact that I was stoned.

It was still early when I woke. My bladder was bursting and my urge to piss was giving me a hard-on. The Plaza de España was slowly beginning to fill with people. I bought a peseta's worth of doughnuts. In the toilet of the Café de España my piss shot up like a fountain, wetting my hand and my trousers. I ordered a milky coffee. The café was used by people waiting for buses. Mr Abdullah's café wasn't open yet.

I caught a bus to Hayy Jadid, which was where I would find the Mu'tamid ben 'Abbad School. The area was pretty desolate—all cactus and scrub and dust and garbage and wasteland. The housing there consisted mainly of tin shacks or brick-built huts, occupied by bedouin whose appearance was as grim as their tattered clothes. I watched their children shit and piss right next to the huts, as if it was the most normal thing in the world.

When I asked the school janitor if I could talk to the headmaster, he asked:

'Why?'

'I've got a letter for him.'

'Let me see.'

'It's a personal letter and I'm supposed to deliver it to him in person.'

He gave me a look that suggested I'd insulted him and then disappeared. Either he'd gone to consult the headmaster or he was pretending to. Eventually he came back and led me along to the headmaster's office. I handed over my letter of recommendation. The envelope had got crumpled in my pocket. The headmaster asked me to sit down as he began reading the letter. I could see that he was smiling. What was he smiling at? Had Hassan played some kind of practical joke on me? At length he laid the letter on top of a stack of files and asked:

'Where are you from?'

'The Rif.'

'And where do your parents live?'

'My mother lives in Tetuan, but I moved to Tangier, because I wanted to find a job.'

'And your father?'

'He's dead.'

My father had died in the summer of 1979, at the age of 22.

'Where are you working in Tangier?'

The moment of truth was approaching.

'I do any work I can get.'

'What do you mean, any work you can get?'

'I work at anything I can lay my hands on.'

'Have you ever been to school before?'

He had the accent of someone from the mountains.

'No.'

I'd fallen into a trap. I blushed fiercely. Hassan hadn't warned me that I was going to be subjected to an interrogation like this. 'Just give the headmaster this letter and he'll enrol you... No problem...' That was what he'd said. I could feel beads of sweat breaking out on my forehead and sweat trickling from my armpits.

'I'm sorry. I'm afraid I'm not in a position to offer you a place at the school. You'd be better off returning to Tangier. There at least you'll be able to carry on earning a living.'

'But I *want* to go to school. I hate the kind of work I've been doing in Tangier.'

He folded his arms on the desk and took another look at my letter. Then he glanced up again.

'How old are you?'

'Twenty.'

'Do you know what your friend Hassan was doing here in Larache a few days ago?'

'No.'

'They found him drunk in the mosque with a friend of his. The two of them have now been expelled from the Institute.'

He needn't worry about me, I thought. I wouldn't fuck about. Hassan had dropped me right in it! Later I found out that he and his friend had also been dossing in the upstairs room of the mosque, which is where students sleep when they have no grants and nowhere else to live.

I answered the headmaster with an air of injured innocence:

'I'm not like Hassan.' (He smiled.) 'I didn't know he did things like that. What he did there was wrong, it was sacrilegious...'

To be honest, I didn't give a shit about what he'd done in Larache. All he'd told me in Tangier was: 'I'm going to Tetuan;

then I'm going back to Larache.'

'I'm sorry,' said the headmaster. 'You see, we have a problem here. The reception class is for young boys and you're almost a man. You're old enough to shave already. And anyway, what the older boys should be doing is memorizing the Koran and Ibn 'Ashir.'

He was right about the shaving. And I had hair growing in other places too, which I needn't go into...

I reached up instinctively and felt my face. I hadn't shaved for days, although up to then I'd been shaving pretty regularly.

'I'll study as hard as I can. I really want to get on in school, and I'll shave every day.'

I was thinking, the Prophets were pretty lucky. They didn't need anyone to teach them—everything came to them in a revelation, ready-packaged. The rest of us aren't so lucky. We have to sit and learn like monkeys.

The headmaster replied, in a quiet but deadly tone:

'I'm sorry.'

The bell rang for break-time. Through the open office window I could see the school yard and the students racing to the toilets, pushing and jostling each other out of the way. I imagined myself as one of their number. I was well aware that having missed out on my schooling was a big loss.

An unpleasant-looking man arrived, carrying some papers. He must have been the maths teacher. The headmaster asked him to take me and give me an arithmetic test. The day of judgement had arrived! I followed him to an empty classroom. He gave me a piece of chalk and dictated a list of numbers which I was supposed to write on the blackboard. The trouble was, I didn't know how to write numbers with zeros in the middle. I just about managed to fake it, though. Then he dictated more numbers, which I was supposed to put underneath the first lot, in a row. He told me to add them up. Then he dictated another list of numbers and told me to subtract them from the first batch. Till then, I'd only ever done these kinds of sums in my head. Then he dictated more numbers, and just to make it harder he put more zeros in the middle!

We went back to the headmaster's office. I didn't like this teacher at all. I felt exhausted—like I'd made an enormous effort. I'd probably have found it easier to hump a 50-kilo load for a kilometre down the road rather than do sums like these.

At this point someone else joined me and the headmaster in the office. He was wearing a *djellaba.* Speaking in Spanish, he asked my name, my place of birth, my age, and various things about Tangier and the kind of work I'd been doing there. I answered as best I could. He had a sympathetic air about him:

'Where did you learn Spanish?'

'From our neighbours, the gypsies, and from the Andalusians in Tetuan and Tangier.'

He wasn't glaring at me like the maths teacher had. I decided that he was probably the Spanish teacher. The headmaster asked him to give me an oral test, which he did. Then they asked me to come back the following day.

I walked back into town. I decided not to take the main asphalt road, but a side road that led off it. The road was sandy and dusty, and my feet sank into the sand. Along the road there were hedges of cactus, clusters of huts with half-naked, barefoot children outside them, ugly, emaciated stray dogs, and chickens foraging in the shit.

At the end of the street there was a disused well. I went over to it. As I stared down into its dark, silent depths, I had a sudden urge to hurl myself head-first down the shaft. The silence seemed to awaken all the despair within me. It was a silence of eternity. Next to the well was a large stone that was so heavy I could hardly lift it. I picked it up, heaved it over the edge and dropped it down the shaft. I listened as it crashed to the dry bottom of the well. Then there was silence. I stared down into the gloom and smelt the vile smell coming up from the bottom, like a festering pit. I moved away from the mouth of the well. I could still hear the crash of the falling stone ringing in my ears. I imagined myself falling in the same way. But unlike the stone, I knew that I would have slowly bled to death at the bottom of the well. A horrible way to die. I set off on my way again. There was something about the sound of that falling stone—a siren call that was still strangely attractive to me. I found myself having to resist it until eventually these gloomy fantasies were dispelled by the sight of a tree. I went across and stretched out under its leafy shade.

I remembered the story of a young man who had hurled himself over the cliffs in Tangier harbour. His mother was from the countryside around Fahs and she had come to town to find her son's grave. When she explained her problem to the man in charge of the cemetery, he said:

'I'm afraid I can't help you. I've no idea where his grave is. You see—we've got a huge number of people buried here... You'll have to go to the registrar's office, that's where they keep the records... Explain how your son died. They might be able to tell you the number of his grave.'

'Ah, what times we live in! My poor Abdelwahid! Is that all that's left of him—a number...? Which they *might* be able to tell me...!'

Poor woman. She raised her tired, toil-marked face to the heavens, weeping and begging Allah to forgive her son his sins. She wept and wailed, until eventually she fainted. Then, still obsessed with her son's fate, she returned to her village.

And I remembered that my mother too had endured her share of sufferings. I remembered her praying for me and begging Allah to protect me from adversity.

2

The Masters Run Away and Their Servants Die

A small but unforgettable event in Morocco's recent history.

Workmen and passers-by were gathering in the Plaza de España. There was the sound of voices shouting excitedly:

'Down with the pasha!'[1]

'Down with traitors!'

The crowd began running towards the pasha's house, shouting:

'Down with the pasha! Down with the pasha!'

The local pasha had gone to Souq Thalatha el Raysana and made a speech there to an audience of peasants. They hadn't liked the speech and when they began booing him, throwing stones at him and threatening him with sticks, his bodyguard had opened fire.

'Listen to him! The way he's talking, you'd think Independence never happened!'

'They look like a swarm of ants...'

The demonstration began to form up: men, women and children. The march was stewarded by supporters of the new regime. They got the crowd ready to set off while the chanting of slogans against the pasha continued. The stewards were wearing armbands, bearing

---

1. The pasha was an agent of Spanish colonialism.

the colours of the Moroccan flag, as confirmation of their authority.[1]

'There's not a policeman in sight!'

'I don't think the police will come. They've probably had orders to maintain a low profile and not get involved. These days everyone knows that the pasha's opposed to independence.'

Then children started shouting slogans against the pasha, jeering and booing, copying the grown-ups. They rushed around, yelling, and stabbing imaginary people with imaginary swords. They drew on a small arsenal of make-believe weapons and played at killing people: they threw stones up into the air, pretending they were grenades: boom... boom... boom...! They had sticks, which they brandished like knives, and guns, clubs, shotguns and machine guns... They looked even more aggressively militant than the grown-ups.

The march came to a halt in front of the pasha's house, and a loud cheer went up:

'Come out and give yourselves up!'

There was a burst of gunfire from one of the windows of the house.[2] Somebody was firing into the air. The crowd retreated at a run, but then a voice shouted:

'Don't be afraid. They're only trying to scare us!'

One of the new government's supporters had a revolver and another was carrying an old shotgun. They went up into a couple of houses opposite the pasha's house and began shooting back.

---

1. In Tangier, in the period immediately after Independence, some of the supporters of the new regime took to wearing military-style uniforms. Some had complete uniforms, while others only had single items, such as caps, jackets or trousers. Depending on what they could lay their hands on, they wore air force, army or navy uniforms, with officer's insignia and bearing the Moroccan national flag. The uniforms were often acquired from sailors on US warships in exchange for traditional Moroccan handicrafts. The authorities did nothing to prevent this happening. All kinds of things were permitted in that period.

2. In the end it turned out that the only person actually in the house was Rabeh, who was well known in town as the pasha's servant. People had thought that the pasha was still in the house, but they later discovered that he had fled to Spain, with his Spanish wife, via Tetuan and Sebta, under the protection of the Spanish authorities (a protection which extended to cutting telephone comunications between Larache and Tetuan on the day in question).

People scattered and fled, but soon crept back again. A contingent of Spanish soldiers came and lined up on the pavement near the pasha's house, with a captain in charge. Somebody said:

'They're scared. They've got no authority to use firearms on us. They're just trying to frighten us. We'll burn them out...!'

People arrived carrying a can of petrol. They used it to set fire to the pasha's garage. The shooting from the pasha's house stopped and a door opened. There stood the pasha's manservant, with his gun raised above his head. He was a black man. The mob began shouting:

'Rabeh! Rabeh! It's Rabeh!'

The captain in charge of the Spanish soldiers tried to stop the crowd from attacking the pasha's servant, but by now they were going wild. They pounced on him. Rabeh threw his gun to the ground, in a gesture of surrender. He already had blood on his face. Not a sound came from his lips. They buried their nails into his flesh and tore at his clothing. They leapt on him with clubs. He staggered under the weight of their wild, brutish blows until finally he collapsed. An army of people fell on him, hacking at him with whatever came to hand. They dragged him down to the street. The women were shrieking with joy. The children were rushing around, yelling with excitement. One man stepped out of the crowd, and it was as if he had all the mob's craziness concentrated inside him. He smashed a bottle of petrol over Rabeh's head. Another man soaked the end of a stick in petrol, set fire to it and threw it onto him. The crowd was going wild with excitement in this primal ritual celebration. Amid the sounds of rejoicing, angry voices were shouting at their victim:

'Die, you dirty dog...'

'Die, you bastard...'

'Die, dog! Die, dog!'

As he rolled and writhed on the ground, his body burned like a kind of terrible flaming torch. Then he lay still. There was a nauseating smell of burning human flesh. A charred, mangled lump of humanity. They hacked at it with knives and cleavers, and even tore at it with their nails. A woman snatched up one of the leg bones, which still had some flesh on it. She bit into it dementedly and then wrapped it in a piece of cloth that she'd torn from her clothes. Slipping the bundle under her arm, she disappeared.

'What's she going to do with it?'

'She'll use it to put a spell on her husband, to stop him beating her, or divorcing her, or running off with other women. That's what they're saying.'

Within a few minutes all that was left of the body was a few charred remains and a gut-wrenching smell of burnt human flesh. Then they went into the house and began dragging out furniture and piling it up in the street. They set fire to some of the furniture and the pasha's paperwork. Burning and looting. The government men seemed alarmed at this and shouted:

'Don't burn the books. We'll take them to party headquarters.'[1]

By this time clouds of smoke were billowing out of the house. The ululations of the women demonstrators and the shouts of excited children echoed round about. The town's Spanish inhabitants were watching all this from the windows and balconies of their homes, in silence. The Spanish soldiers stayed put, not moving off the pavement.

Then some of the demonstrators ran off, splitting up into groups as they went. Their chosen targets were the houses of various of the pasha's agents in town. A jeep and a truck arrived and began loading what was left of the paperwork and the more valuable items of furniture that hadn't been burned. Then the government men put a cordon across the street, to stop people stealing furniture and taking it home with them. One man was actually taking his clothes off in the street and putting on clothes from a pile that had been looted.

The mob broke into the house of one of the pasha's agents in Calle Barcelona, but they found nobody there. Again, burning and looting. Then they continued on their rampage, storming round to the houses of anyone they suspected of being a traitor[2] to the nation.

1. The Independence Party.

2. On this particular day, it was enough for one of the demonstrators to accuse someone of treason for that person to be burned. The old man who was burned at the stake (Sharif el Soumati) had been the headman of the village of Qiryat Khamis el Saahil. It was later claimed that one of the demonstrators had owed him money and, since he couldn't afford to pay, had used this as a way of getting rid of him.

An angry mob appeared from the direction of Bab el Kubaybat. They had an old man in their clutches and were dragging him roughly along the ground, stabbing at him with knives. The old man had lost most of his clothes by this time. His eyes were starting out of his head. This mass of moving flesh had entirely lost its humanity. Somebody brought some rope and they tied him to a tree by his arms and legs in front of Bab el Kubaybat, effectively crucifying him. They tipped petrol over him and put a match to it. Again, there were shrieks and screams of joy, and people leaping in the air. The smell of burning flesh began to spread across Plaza de España. The old man's eyes bulged out of his head and began rolling around in their sockets.

His body twitched convulsively. The Spanish woman who ran the wine shop next to Bab el Kubaybat, directly opposite the scene of the crucifixion, screamed:

'My God...! No! No! No...!'

Then she passed out. They say that she died of a heart attack.

That night the streets were deserted except for a group of soldiers collecting up the remnants of what had been looted from the pasha's house and the houses of his agents. Two vehicles pulled up next to the tree: a police car and an ambulance. The ambulance men wore masks and rubber gloves. They gathered up the last remaining fragments of flesh and bone and put them in a box, while the police guarded the rest of the square. They sprayed a kind of powder on the ground and on the charred remains of the tree—it filled the square with a vile, choking smell. But the smell of human flesh proved stronger and lingered in people's nostrils.

3

My First Lesson

On my first day at the new school, the headmaster escorted me into the classroom and introduced me to the teacher:

'Mr Mohamed, this is the young man who will be studying with you.'

They stepped outside the door for a moment, to talk about something—presumably about me. I'm convinced that the headmaster put me into that class in order to test me. If I didn't make the grade, after a few days he'd be telling me:

'You don't seem to be cut out for studying here. It'd be better for you to return to Tangier.'

The other pupils started whispering together and looking me up and down. I felt very peculiar standing there in front of them. I'd never been in front of forty people before, all of them examining me from head to toe. The pupils in the class were all about my age, but they already knew how to read and write. There was a written lesson on the blackboard, and they had their exercise books open in front of them. I later discovered that most of them were country kids.

The teacher came back into the room and sat me in the middle row, next to the smallest boy in the class. There were three rows of seats in the classroom. In the front row, just to my right, there were four plump girl pupils.

The teacher said:

'This is a new arrival in the class. I want you to help him settle in.'

They carried on staring at me, whispering and fidgeting in their seats. The teacher rapped the desk with his ruler, and they went quiet. Most of them were wearing *djellabas*. They all looked as if they were short of sleep. It was easy enough to pick out the country kids from the town kids, from their faces and the way they dressed.

They were copying the written lesson from the blackboard. What on earth were they copying? In front of me sat an exercise book and a pencil, waiting for me to start my first lesson. Hand-written letters—the 'symbols of the world'—were slowly materializing in my deskmate's book, but my pages stayed obstinately blank. I stared at my classmates, impressed by their handwriting. Would the headmaster let me learn to write like that? If he didn't, then I'd have no choice but to return to live a life of professional depravity in Tangier, never having learned how to interpret what happens in this world by means of its symbols. Since I'd come this far, I was determined to learn. In Tangier somebody had once told me, 'True life is always to be found in books.'

The teacher strolled slowly round the class, looking at some of the kids' classwork, until he arrived at my desk. A calm, friendly man, who presumably didn't spend his time hanging out with street kids. He leaned over my exercise book and wrote some words on the second page, each word on a separate line, and quietly pronounced each of the words in turn. Then he asked me to copy the words until each line was full. My small, timid deskmate kept glancing across at me, and at the feeble handwriting in my exercise book, as I struggled with the words. My hand was trembling with the effort of all this writing, but the fact that he was watching me meant that I tried not to shake so much. By now I'd filled three whole lines. I folded my arms and watched the teacher walking between the rows, and then I looked at the others copying out their lesson. Some of them had finished already. The teacher came over to see what I had written:

'Good! You'll soon get the hang of this, God willing.'

Then he asked my deskmate to write out more words for me, which he did. The rest of the class were still whispering and muttering about me, but the teacher stood up and surveyed them with a stern expression. They all fell silent. I could tell by the look on my friend's face that he was happy—certainly happier than I was... Compared with the rest of them, I felt horribly inferior. The only alphabet I knew was the few letters that Hamid had taught me in Tangier. I felt wretched and guilty, as if I had no right to be there. I had come from a clan of pimps, thieves, smugglers and prostitutes. I felt as if I was in a sacred place, defiling it by my presence—even though, as it turned out, a lot of these kids came from the same kind of sordid background as me. I was depressed and I wrestled with whether I should stay there or return to Tangier. But I knew that Tangier was no bed of roses and that staying at the school would be better for me in the long run.

My deskmate wrote out more words for me, pronouncing each of them in a low voice, just as the teacher had done. I thanked him. My hand trembled again as I settled down to work, trying to copy his neat handwriting. From that moment on, I found that I was learning more from my fellow students than from the teachers.

4

In the Dining Hall

There was always a mad scramble to get the best places in the dining hall. The teachers would take it in turns to supervise us at breakfast and lunch, doing one week at a time. The girls always lined up and went in before us. They weren't what you'd call good-looking, but one of them wasn't bad. Their giggling and whispering mingled with the clatter of spoons and dishes. The teacher on lunch duty would patrol up and down inside the dining room. Occasionally he'd go and stand outside the door, turning his back on us and staring out into the empty space of the schoolyard. This was the signal for the noise to start, echoing round the hall, until eventually the teacher would come back in and start shouting at us:

'Any of you donkeys... who don't want to keep quiet and eat... can leave the hall right now!'

Then he'd go back to smoking his cigarette in the doorway. This was the same unpleasant teacher who'd tested me in arithmetic on my first day.

The mark of poverty was written on all our faces. We had nothing more than our humanity and the clothes we stood up in. Maybe once the girls grew up and got settled, they'd be beautiful, who knows!

The first course was usually lentils, and we'd find it waiting for us on the tables. There were usually flies in the food, sometimes alive and sometimes dead, and you'd have to pick them out before you could start eating. Some of the kids thought that the flies had a germ in one wing, and something to kill the germs in their other wing, and that explained why they'd sometimes crash-land in your dinner. They invented these kinds of stories to make up for their wretched lives.

I deliberately used to sit at the end of the hall because that gave me a chance to steal pieces of bread from the tables in the first row. There was never enough food for us older boys. We even went round picking up crumbs. If any of the pupils were feeling ill, whether they were there or not, we took advantage of their loss of appetite to grab their portions. We always ate the first course warily because there were usually bits of grit in it. I remember one of the boys chewing on a splinter of glass in a bowl of rice and ending up spitting blood. The second course was usually fried egg, fish in a tomato sauce, or pieces of so-called meat. The meat was usually rubbery or rock solid, and we were always scared to swallow it in case it got stuck in our throats. Usually we'd just chew it as best we could, suck out the juices and then spit it out. The main ingredients of every school meal were lentils and greens.

Once I went and caught four flies outside the school. I wrapped them in a piece of paper, intending to drop them into the plates of other kids sitting next to me. Sometimes I even went hunting for flies in the toilets—after all, there's no such thing as a clean fly or a dirty fly. When I was dropping these flies into other people's bowls, I had to make sure that the teacher didn't see me. Some of my fellow pupils saw me, but they didn't tell on me.

However, the teacher did catch me stealing a piece of bread. He hit me and barred me from the dining hall for three days. The other kids stuck by me, and brought me out slices of bread and bits of fish and meat from their own meals. This teacher was a stickler for the rules—there wasn't much compassion in him.

Because we were poor, we respected each other and we stuck together. Almost all of us knew the experience of poverty—a poverty which our exploiters considered a normal, natural fact of life.

After all the battling over lunch, I generally fancied a sleep to make up for what I'd missed out on during the night. There was a concrete bench outside, butting up against one wall of the school, and that was where I slept. Sometimes I slept so soundly that I missed a lesson or even a whole afternoon.

Near the school lived a cripple who was better at maths than any of the students. He was probably better than some of the teachers too, according to what I'd heard. He'd dropped out of junior school and hadn't taken the entrance exam for secondary school. His mother had died, and his father had left town years ago and never returned. Not so much as a word as to his whereabouts. He'd left his crippled son in the care of a maternal aunt, who was deaf and dumb, and who earned her living by searching through rubbish piles early in the morning and by begging at the bus station.

The cripple used to help the students with their maths homework. The kids would cluster round him, putting their questions, and he would show them various ways of solving their problems. In return for his help with their homework, they gave him a few coins, or single cigarettes, or food, or whatever they had. Sometimes they'd organize a sweepstake among themselves, on the answer to one of the problems. The winner would share the takings with the cripple. Even though he was always helping like this, he never asked for anything in return. When luck brought a few pesetas my way, I used to buy him Virginia cigarettes because he preferred them to black tobacco. I bought them from the street sellers in town, who sold them singly if you asked them.

There was a Christian graveyard nearby and I used to enjoy sitting in it. I used to wander around between the rows of graves. I enjoyed reading the names and trying to decipher the words on the tombstones, even the ones I couldn't understand. I don't know what it is that attracts me to graveyards. Is it the atmosphere of peace and calm? Or is it a habit left over from the days when I used to sleep in graveyards? Or is it perhaps a craving for death?[1]

I used to enjoy going out to a field not far from the school. I'd

---

1. This habit has stayed with me right up to the present day. Some of my writings (including the first section of my autobiography *For Bread Alone* and a few chapters of this present book) were written as I sat on graves in Jewish, Christian and Moslem graveyards. My favourites are the graves that date from nineteenth-century Tangier. I find them particularly impressive.

lie in the shade of a tree smoking dog-ends that I'd picked up in town, since I was completely broke. I used to lie there watching the passing clouds and imagining them as splendid mythical creatures. Or I'd recall the best of the good times in Tangier: memories of thighs, and women's bellies, and beautiful breasts, and then I'd masturbate. This flood of memories would send me off to sleep, and by the time I woke up it felt as if I'd been asleep for hours.

5

When Lice Burn, They Smell of Human Flesh

Hassan arrived back from Tetuan. He'd been to the local office of the education ministry, to sort out the problem about his re-admission to the Institute. We started hanging out with five or six of the Zailachi boys in Mr Abdullah's café. They were all students at the Institute. Some of them were lucky—they had scholarships. The rest had no grants at all. At the end of each week, some of them got food parcels from their families; the rest went home for the weekend.

Hassan had no kind of support from his family. He and his brothers had bankrupted their father's business years ago, and they'd shared out between them what remained after his death. Hassan had the idea of buying small items from local wholesalers—reels of thread, needles, boxes of chocolate and so on—and he went round selling them to the small shops, in the Kubaybat and elsewhere. I went with him once. He'd bought some reels of thread from a Jewish trader, and then went on to sell them to a Moroccan shop just a few yards down the road at twice the price he'd paid for them.

We smoked *kif* because it was cheaper than cigarettes and more powerful. I was pretty much dependent on the customers in the café, all of whom were poor like us. They helped me with my homework and taught me extra bits about the subjects I was studying. Hassan taught me the art of putting basic sentences together. It was heavy going, but he never complained. I was doing good work in my written pieces, but I knew that I was making a lot of mistakes. When I asked him to explain the rules of grammar, he said:

'Don't worry about the case endings for the nominative and the accusative and so on. The most important thing is to learn the basics of reading and writing. Even people who know all the rules of grammar make mistakes when they're reading and writing, so don't bother about it too much.'

I wondered at the time whether Hassan was telling the truth, or whether he was just covering up the fact that he knew nothing about grammar. Later I discovered that what he said was true.

Miloudi helped me in checking through my Spanish, which he knew better than Arabic. He was one of the laziest students in the Institute and also the heaviest *kif* smoker among us.

I was permanently hungry. The hunger pangs were worst in the evening—I felt the effects in a general slowness and confusion, and a heavy beating of my heart. The school food at lunchtime was never enough to last me till nightfall. Smoking the *kif* only made me hungrier, but on the other hand it helped to anaesthetize my fears and anxieties. In the mornings I was often late for the school breakfast because I'd overslept. Because I was cold and hungry, and because I was scratching my dirty skin and my hair, I often found it hard to get to sleep at night. When the night of the lucky ones ended—the ones who'd been out for the evening—that was when *my* night began. Usually some of my fellow students kept back pieces of bread for me, and I lived on bread and water, because I had nothing else to eat.

The journey between the school and the town centre was a good quarter of an hour's walk. On winter days, it was horribly depressing. In the evenings I went to a charitable refuge—another fifteen-minute walk. I wasn't officially registered for eating in the canteen there, but the beadle had taken pity on me. He used to give me small pieces of bread dipped in gravy, or with a slice of meat, a piece of fat or a fried sardine. Sometimes it rained on my return route and the only available shelter was under a tree, but the drips from its branches just made me even wetter. Sometimes the beadle wasn't there, so I'd have to go away hungrier than ever, cursing anyone I saw eating.

Once I went to the refuge at Friday lunchtime. Now, couscous is a food I've never liked, and I usually try to avoid it—probably because this was what the mourners had eaten (with tripe) after my uncle's funeral in the Rif, during the days of famine. I was seven at the time. On this particular occasion the beadle asked me to join the other hostel residents for lunch, so I found myself sitting at a table with four old people. The sight of their senility and decrepitude filled me with disgust, although, to be honest, they were more deserving of pity: one of them had an eye missing; another was dribbling; another had no teeth; and the fourth had hands that trembled and shook. Not to mention various other disabilities. I felt that their deformities somehow reflected on me. That was the first and last time that I ate there.

It was couscous for lunch. The four old people looked at me as they devoured their food greedily and noisily. I was overcome with a sense of shame, I suppose because I wasn't actually suffering from physical disabilities myself. The server put a plate in front of me. I ate the vegetables quickly, but I didn't touch the couscous, or the strip of meat, which was tough and rubbery and not cut up like in the school canteen. The others chewed and chewed, and finally swallowed the meat. I wondered how they could ever hope to digest it. I got out my handkerchief and, pretending to wipe my mouth, spat the rubbery lump into it. The beadle gave me a piece of plain bread for my supper, and I left.

My stomach was heaving so much that I almost threw up before I reached the front door. On the way back to town I couldn't stop thinking about their faces. They looked more like cavemen. Ugly and deformed. The thought of them disgusted me. I felt cramps in my stomach. I went over to a tree and spewed the entire contents of my guts, vomiting it up until all I had left to vomit was air. My eyes were watering and I felt dizzy. I sat and rested for a while before setting off again. Luckily, that evening Salahami was kind enough to give me a bit of fish to put into the piece of bread the beadle had given me.

My longings for my cursed Tangier were making me miserable. Even the worst of situations there would be better than what I was living here. It was a strange fact, but no sooner had I left Tangier —heartily sick of it—than I'd become obsessed with a longing for it.

My clothes were scruffy and dirty, and I knew that I smelt bad. I had lice nesting in my clothes. My shoes were letting in water. My hair was dirty and sticky, and had grown long. It was so itchy that I was forever scratching my head. One day, as I sat and scratched, I noticed something small and black under one of my nails. I combed my hair forwards to clean out the dust and scurf, and the combing produced a lively black louse. Each combing produced three or four more of the plump little creatures. They were pretty energetic, so I poked them with a twig to see if I could get them to race each other. Then I wrapped them in a scrap of paper and set fire to them to amuse myself with the popping sound as they burned.

6

The Tears of the Three Lovers

I stayed in the café till it closed at around midnight. Then I roamed the streets waiting for Bab Allah (the big mosque) to open for the dawn prayers. When the mosque opened, I went in, found a damp-smelling mat in one corner and curled up on it—no chance of sleeping, though. I kept being woken up by the people coming in to pray. In the end the mosque attendant came over to me and said:

'This isn't a flop-house. It's a place of prayer and worship.'

I pleaded with him to leave me alone. When he persisted, I started shouting at him, cursing his mother and his whole family, and then went out into the alley again, my shoes in my hand. It was still early morning. I'd just found myself a corner next to a building where I could curl up and sleep when all of a sudden I felt someone stumble and fall on top of me. I cursed angrily. It turned out to be the blind *mukhtar*, Haddad.

I'd heard of him. He'd studied at the Religious Institute and he had a reputation as a brilliant student, particularly in the Arabic tradition and its origins. He'd memorized the Koran and the *hadith*, as well as a lot of Arabic poetry, both sacred and secular.

He started apologizing profusely. I sat him down next to me and told him not to worry about it. I was still very sleepy, but his presence overcame my desire to sleep. When he heard I was studying at the Institute, he pulled out a book from beneath his woollen *djellaba—The Tears of the Three Lovers* by Zaki Mubarak. He suggested that we went together to the Café Central, saying that he'd treat me to breakfast and we could read the book together. It was Sunday. As we sat there outside the mosque, I told him a little about my life and the circumstances that had led me to start college in Larache. We became friends there and then. At every word which either of us said, he would let out a long sigh. He was poor too, but he wasn't a homeless orphan like myself. He wasn't forever having slanging matches with his father. He had an elder brother, who supported the family, and a younger brother who was studying. I think God must have been pleased with our encounter. Several times the *mukhtar* declared to me, in good Arabic:

'Things are hard now, but they'll get easier as you go along...'

He was amazingly clever at finding his way round the streets and pavements. When we needed to cross the road, he'd stop me at the kerb and glance left and right, as if it was him leading me, and not the other way round. Then he'd say:

'Alright, we can cross now...'

He actually saw with his ears. I let him carry on as usual, as if he was on his own. We bought *shurus* and then we went to the Café Central. After we'd had breakfast, I settled down and began reading from *The Tears of the Three Lovers*. If I found a word too hard to pronounce, he encouraged me to read it carefully, getting me to repeat it several times. He explained:

'Arabic is basically a phonetic language.'

Here I'm talking about 1957—years later, in the 1980s, I found myself reading a book entitled *Arabs are a Phonetic Phenomenon*.

He could handle grammar and knew how to conjugate all the difficult verbs. This was the kind of man I wanted for a teacher. To hell with teachers who have no patience for teaching!

At that time I was reading anything I could lay my hands on: books that I'd bought or borrowed; and any item of printed matter that I happened to find on the ground. Mostly in Spanish. I developed a passion for reading. I'd even copy down the signs over shops and cafés. I'd write them on scraps of paper or in my notebook. They were mostly in Spanish too. I was more than ready to learn, even though I could have wished for better circumstances.

Rimbaud was right when he said:

'It's not healthy to go wearing out your trousers on a school bench, studying.'

Wise words!

Reading and writing had become a sleeping and waking obsession with me. Sometimes I imagined myself as a big letter or as a pen. On occasion I didn't have the price of a new exercise book, so I picked up paper off the street and wrote my lessons on that. Sometimes it was paper which previously had *shurus* wrapped in it and the writing would disappear in patches of grease... words arranged strangely, here and there. I used to enjoy the way these patterns appeared on the sheet. My dirtiness and my hunger made me forget about bodily pleasures, as if they were now a thing of the past. God, what a miserable way to spend your time!

In the elementary class we had a young teacher, whose job it was to teach us Arabic. He fancied himself. He spent more time worrying about his looks than about what he was supposed to be teaching us. He'd parade between the rows of desks as if, in his mind's eye, he was walking in the street, eyeing up the girls. From time to time he would pause to straighten the knot of his tie in the reflection from the window. If the window wasn't open, he'd open it. He'd often tell us jokes or ask one of us to tell a joke. He laughed at the stupidest things. He was in the habit of pulling out a book or a newspaper and reading it in class, and sometimes he'd ask us to do our classwork in silence so as not to disturb his reading. I used to wonder about this beardless brown monkey—was he there to teach us or to study us?

He had a flaming temper, too, and if any of us made the slightest mistake, he'd start ranting at us. In his opinion, we were all donkeys and he was riding us, with the aid of his superior knowledge and the cane that he kept lying on his desk. He'd hit anyone who made him angry. His victims would cringe and hop about, and then return to their seats in tears. He took a particular dislike to me and amused himself making fun of my weaknesses in Arabic. Once, I'd been supposed to learn a poem off by heart, but I hadn't done it. It was by Safieddin el Huli, and began with these lines:

Travel, because you will always find a replacement for what

> you have left behind.
>
> And do something. The good thing about life is to be doing things.
>
> I have seen that stillness spoils water. Running water tastes good, while standing water does not.

He came across to me angrily and lashed my shoulder three times with his thin cane. At the third blow, the tip of the cane caught my left ear. He was picking on me in particular because I was older than the other boys in the class. He ended his angry ape-like outburst with these words:

'Idiot... Donkey... Don't you want to study? Why don't you just go back to Tangier with your market friends instead of wasting your time here, and us wasting our time on you?'

However, that was the only time he actually hit me. After that he confined himself to insulting me, until in the end he seemed to forget that I was there. I reached up and felt the blood on my ear. There was a loathing in the eyes of my classmates. They were on my side. I thought of pouncing on him and fighting him, as I used to in Tetuan or Tangier, even if I was the one who came off worse. I imagined us fighting until one of us gave up, and me biting one of his stupid donkey ears off and spitting it in his face. But I didn't want to be thrown out of the school. So I'd leave his donkey ears for some other donkey to bite. When the lesson ended, I went to the toilets and rinsed the dried blood from my ear. Drops of blood had fallen onto my shoulder. As I washed my ear, the blood began flowing again.

We had another teacher—the one who'd given me the maths test on my first day at the school. He had a foul temper, just like the other teacher, and he used to call us donkeys too. He always carried a couple of books with him, usually in a foreign language. I heard that he was studying English by correspondence and that he spoke Spanish and a little French. He taught us maths, history and geography. He used to cane us too, on our fingertips, and sometimes he'd hit us. But on the other hand he was fair, in the sense that he never ended a lesson without talking things over with the person he'd punished. We didn't despise him in the same way that we despised his colleague. In fact he actually went out of his way to help some of the poorer pupils from the countryside with money and clothing, and he'd visit them in their homes to make sure they were alright. However his compassion and his concern outside school didn't extend to me.

I had no place to live and no place to sleep. At night I used to hang out with the drunks and the hash smokers and the night-walkers. There was always a place for me with them. They were like each other and they helped each other, wherever they were, at any time and in any place. But if anyone wasn't prepared to share their way of life, then they rejected them.

I was slowly beginning to be able to read and understand 'the world's symbols'. Eventually I passed the entry exam for secondary school. During the maths exam I cheated by copying from another pupil. Somebody told me that some of the students got through by bribery or by using influence, so I felt justified in doing a bit of cheating myself. Once school was over, the restaurant owner Salahami gave me the price of a bus ticket and I returned to Tangier. My cursed city! Yet I still loved it, even after all that time.

7

El Murwani

El Murwani came to the Café Ballerina as usual, except that on this particular day he wasn't carrying the large tray filled with the flat, Pakistani-style loaves that he usually sold round the popular cafés. This time he was only carrying rolls, spread with butter and honey. As he ate his breakfast, he started ranting that 'certain people' had been talking about him behind his back, accusing him of being a traitor to his country. He finished his breakfast, and then began shouting in an angry voice:

'I'll show them, today... I'll show them who's a so-called agent of imperialism...!'

The other customers looked at each other nervously because they could see the craziness in his eyes. He took out a cigarette and smoked it, looking extremely agitated. Then, from under his white flowing gown, he suddenly produced a large knife. The customers froze. Their faces twitched imperceptibly as they sat glued to their seats. He glared round the café. All eyes were on him and nobody dared so much as blink.

'Today the bastards are going to find out who I *really* am!'

He put the knife back in his belt and went running out in the direction of ‘Aqbat el Siyaghin. In Plaza Benito Pérez Galdós[1] he pulled the knife out and used it to stab a Jewish money-changer in his shop. Then he stabbed a woman tourist. He ran down Tariq el Touahin waving the knife, which by now was dripping with blood. He ran into some Moroccans, but chose to ignore them. As he went, people heard him yelling:

‘Holy war, in the name of Allah! You bastards! The curse of Allah on all infidels and unbelievers...!’

Arriving in Houmat Bencharqi, he made a beeline for one particular shop. It was shut, so he started kicking at the door and shouting abusive things about its owner. Then he ran off again. In Calle Dar Debagh he attacked a number of foreign tourists. Then he ran down Avenida de España, near the railway station. A Spanish policeman was on the street. El Murwani ran towards him, brandishing his knife. The policeman saw him coming, pulled out his gun and fired at his legs. El Murwani fell. As he rolled about, with blood running from one leg, he was still cursing ‘the bastards’. An ambulance arrived, together with a police jeep, and a crowd of bystanders gathered to watch.

---

1. A famous Spanish writer (1843–1920).

8

The Stubbornness of Love

I was sitting out in front of the Café Central—the heat was making me sleepy—when I saw her coming up from Tariq el Bahriya. She looked like she'd been moulded into her white, diaphanous blouse and the trousers that clung to her slender body. Young and beautiful, she was. A blonde. A flirtatiousness in the way she walked. A small, slightly snub nose, her hair long and sleek, and her upper lip arched. Her eyes large and inviting. She had the look of a quarrelsome cat. An Asiatic cat.

I wanted her, but I needed to know if she was available, so I followed her. By now I was awake and fully alert.

She turned into Calle Curro Las Once and then went into a house on the square. My suspicions proved to be well-founded: she was a prostitute. I waited till she went upstairs. The lady of the house received me with a smile. This was Lala Ghaliya—a fine woman. She was getting on a bit, but she was still elegant and full of life. Her establishment had an air of something special. Dar Es Salaam, it was called—the House of Peace. From one of the rooms I could hear the sound of laughter and people talking and shouting.

She took me into a small room furnished with nothing much except a Moroccan couch. The smell of incense was everywhere. On the walls hung rugs with scenes from the *Arabian Nights*. I ordered a beer. It was brought by a pretty brunette, short and plump, in a white and purple skirt. She leaned over as she put the bottle on the small table next to me and because her skirt was translucent I could see the strong outline of her thighs in the light of the sun. I thanked her, and she turned and smiled at me.

Lala Ghaliya came and looked in through the door, her tall figure breaking the light of the sun's rays. She greeted me with a radiant smile, cigarette in hand, and then came swishing in, in her brightly coloured *caftan*. I ordered a second beer before I'd finished the first and asked about the girl in the white blouse and trousers. She told me that the price of a night with one of the girls would be 50 pesetas, and I said that was fine. She then brought me a third beer before I'd finished the second. She said that the particular girl I wanted was occupied for the moment. I said I'd be happy to wait. She told me she had two other girls, who were more beautiful. I said I'd leave the choice to her. She called out 'Rabi'a!' and the girl who came in was the pretty brunette who'd brought my beer. We had another couple of beers while she told me she was from Meknes. I said I'd never visited her town. We took our drinks to another room, which had a bed in it. I asked her about the girl I'd wanted originally, the one with the white blouse and trousers. She told me she was from Tangier. Rabi'a's scent was strong and passionate, and so was she.

That evening I spent my time round the wine shops in the Inner Souq. Everyone was talking about the craziness of el Murwani, and his rampage, and his family, and the way madness can be inherited, and about colonialism and how it chooses its agents among people with a disadvantage or a chip on their shoulder, who generally end up as criminals.

As drink began to get the better of me, I became more and more determined. I returned to the brothel and spoke with the procuress Shariouta. She said that the girl—her name was Kunza—was still occupied with other men, and that if I wanted her I'd best come back the following day. Or, if I preferred, she had others who were more beautiful than her.

I told her that Kunza was the one I wanted and I was prepared to pay up to 100 pesetas. She said she'd talk to her. I told her that if she could arrange it, there'd be something in it for her too. At that point Kunza appeared in the reception room, walking proud, like a tigress sated on her prey. Then she disappeared again into the inner sanctum. Shariouta brought me my beer and told me:

'If you take my advice, you won't bother with her. She's the stubborn sort, and unfortunately I can't give her the good knock-about she deserves. Women are stronger than men and this is their time—when men want them. Come back another day. Maybe Allah will show her the right way.'

The following morning I was selling counterfeit watches in the harbour. A decent morning's work—I'd earned myself 30 dollars. In the evening I met Hamid Zailachi skulking round the alleys of the Inner Souq. Apparently he'd come out of prison two days previously. His head was shaved and he was wearing a black, threadbare beret. He looked pale and tense.

'They put me in a cell that stank to high heaven—it had rats coming out of the toilet hole. They kept me in there for three days.'

'Why?'

'Because I refused to clean the toilets. I told them I was sick. The guard had it in for me because I had nothing to bribe him with. That's the usual way you get out of cleaning toilets in prison. I'd gone into the Café Normandie for a drink. They refused to serve me, so I went and pissed on the doorstep. The waiters grabbed me and marched me off to the police. I got a month for it.'

Hamid had begun to think about going back to studying in Larache—if he didn't end up going back to prison because of his wicked ways, picking people's pockets. He was good at it, but he knew that one careless move could see him back behind bars again.

'I don't want to end my life among that kind of people. The ones who pass sentence on you in prison are more vicious than the judges who pass sentence on the outside. Give me the judgement of the judges, any day, and not the judgement of the judged!'

I told him what had happened to me with Kunza.

'She obviously knows you've fallen for her and she's trying to trap you. You should keep away from falling in love with prostitutes. You'll discover that every one of them is trying to take revenge on all men through the particular man she's with. They all believe that it's some man's fault that their lives are a mess. They're all frustrated in love.'

'She's a blonde. Somebody once told me that blondes are all

fickle and flighty by nature.'

He roared with laughter.

'Who ever told you that...?! There's no such thing as one colour of woman who's OK and another who isn't. Even if the colour of their skin is different, they're all the same colour inside. Forget about love and just enjoy the sex. Love is a terrible affliction.'

We went to Tariq el Masihiyin and called in at the Bar El Gallo, which was frequented by both Spaniards and Moroccans. Two Spanish women were drinking and chatting with a Spaniard and a Moroccan. We downed a couple of drinks. After a while the prostitutes' laughter began to get on our nerves, so we left. I gave Hamid 100 pesetas because next day he was planning to visit his family in Azila. I probably wouldn't see him again unless he came to Larache.

I went to the Bar Jacobito. Two glasses of wine. I was obsessed with the idea of returning to Shariouta's place. Rabi'a wouldn't be busy. I thought of her beautiful tanned, naked body and the slight downy fuzz of her back, the warmth of her strong thighs and the powerful smell of her sweat. I imagined myself dressing her in all the silk clothes she could ever want, until my bizarre imaginings had me almost choking with laughter. By this time I was writhing like a snake on a hook. I imagined her undressing and undressing until she was more naked than her nakedness. Hamid was right. Stick with the desire for the bread of thighs and not for the hornet of love. Love is a demon once it gets hold of you. It was going to cost me 150 pesetas for Rabi'a and 50 for Shariouta. This was the price of one scented night in Rabi'a's company.

We had a drink and then went to her room in the Hotel La Balata. We bought a bottle of Martini, three lemons and some lemon-soda. The room was small, the hotel modest, and the night scorching. We sat on the edge of the bed in our underclothes.

'Why are you so keen on getting Kunza into bed?'

'I'm the stubborn sort.'

'You're not in love with her, then...?'

'Let's say I fancy her.'

'She's my friend. I'll have a word with her tomorrow, and she'll sleep with you, and it's not going to cost you a fortune. You see, Kunza is stubborn too. Maybe seeing you has reawakened some painful experience in her.'

'It's alright, you needn't bother. It's not so important now, whether I sleep with her or not.'

We had our drinks in silence, lost in thought. Then we looked at each other.

'Is she in love with anyone?'

'No. She's still waiting for true love.'

'True love?'

'Yes. True love.'

'What do you mean, true love?'

She looked at me, smiling.

'I presume you're joking...'

'Not at all.'

'Everyone knows what true love is, so why don't you?'

'I don't know. Really I don't.'

'Don't tell fibs.'

We were like a couple of kids trying to unravel the secrets of the universe.

I bought some books, by Manfaluti, Gibran Khalil Gibran and Mai Ziadeh. I shut myself away and read as much as I could. I had heard that these authors wrote about love—about true love. I went out to the Restaurant Maria near the hotel, and when I came back I had a bottle of wine and all these books about love. I found some comfort in what Manfalouti, Gibran and Ziadeh were saying, but it struck me that their kind of love was always tinged with death, or endless suffering, or obsession.

I ran into Rabi'a in the Inner Souq. Kunza had moved to Rabi'a's hotel so that they could live together. She asked why I didn't join them. It would be cheaper than my present hotel and I'd be able to take anybody I wanted up to my room. A trap was being set for me—that was my first thought. But I decided to move into the hotel anyway, spurred by curiosity and a devil-may-care recklessness. I took a small room on the roof terrace, facing the sea.

I made friends with the night porter—a young man addicted to *kif* and wine, who was generally stoned at any time of day or night. He had developed a hatred of women because his girlfriend Shama had run off with one of his friends. When he was too stoned to work, I stood in for him—always assuming that the *kif* and the wine didn't knock me out first. Sometimes Kunza would arrive with a client and they'd end up spending the night together; other times they'd come down again after a while. Rabi'a was doing the same in another hotel. I don't know what prevented her doing it in her own hotel, because I thought she had an arrangement with the doorman.

I found that my reading was beginning to lessen my interest in the wine and the *kif*. I also bought *Crazy for Laila* and *Cleopatra* by Ahmed Shawqi. One evening Kunza found me sitting behind the desk in reception reading a stage play—*The Idiot*—and she told me:

'You shouldn't read so much. It'll send you crazy!'

A man was following her.

Kunza was also working in a belly-dancing place as an apprentice dancer. Because of this they called her the 'demon dancer'. One night she came back drunk. The taxi driver had to hold her up to get her into the hotel. She had a half-smoked cigarette hanging from her lips. A black lamé evening dress and a paste-jewel necklace hanging across her breasts. A red rose in her hair. People do the kinds of things at night that they'd never do in the daytime. The driver told me, as he left her:

'If you don't hold her up, she'll keel over.'

The whiteness of her face, neck and arms contrasted with the black of her dress. I left her swaying there while I fetched the key to her room from the board.

'I'm an amazing woman! You don't even know me yet.'

'Allal, the night porter, was out for the count. Fast asleep. I removed her cigarette so it wouldn't burn my face and propped her up. I can still remember the smell of her—a combination of wine, tobacco and strong perfume. I'd only drunk a couple of glasses that night. Drink was beyond my pocket. She wrapped her arms around my neck and we went up the stairs, with her ranting away and me filled with all kinds of sexual thoughts. I threw away her cigarette and she seemed to forget about it. We paused on the stairs so that she could talk with the Spanish consul, who frequented the dance hall and was madly in love with her. A couple of times she flopped down on the stairs and I had to heave her up.

'Come on, you can't sleep here.'

I took off her gold shoes and laid her on the bed, fully dressed. There was a certain splendour in the way she lived her nights. I sat at her feet on the edge of the bed and lit a cigarette. I watched her as she lay there, her breath shallow, lost in an alcoholic haze. Now her beauty was that of a dead woman, the kind of beauty that appealed to the Babylonians and the ancient Greeks. I no longer found her in any sense attractive. The glory was gone—her brightness, her flirtatiousness and her arrogance. Now she was free of all human artifice. Now she existed entirely for herself, for whatever she wanted or didn't want.

I went back to my room and drank a glass of water with lemon juice. I smoked a cigarette and thought about human relationships and how sordid they usually were. I dreamed of a long row of naked men taking it in turns to go to bed with Kunza, and her saying to them:

'Come to me, all of you. My time is the time of all women.'

I fell asleep, and dreamed and dreamed, until the dream of dreams finally awoke me.

I hadn't seen Hamid since we parted. I was spending my days trying to sell things to the sailors off the ships, and business wasn't good. Occasionally I'd pick up some money for taking tourists or sailors to one of the bars or brothels. Rabi'a and Kunza were sleeping with the men.

I read diligently, and sometimes I copied down what I was reading. This way I could get a style of writing into my mind, and get the hang of writing properly even without knowing the rudiments of grammar. This had been Hassan's suggestion. October was approaching. I wasn't saving much money. The bars and the brothels had cleaned me out, in my efforts to forget about Kunza. I filled a big case with clothes I had traded with the sailors off the big cargo ships in exchange for traditional Moroccan handicrafts. I'd bought some of the clothes second-hand in the Souq. I decided that I'd sell them to the pupils in Larache on days when I had no money.

The day before I was due to travel, I invited Rabi'a to come swimming. I suggested that we had lunch at one of the restaurants on the beach. We swam and played and ran about. In my mind's eye I was spitting on Kunza, and in the meantime I was having fun with Rabi'a in the water. We flirted with each other. We played a game that involved one of us standing in the water with our legs apart, and the other person swimming through. Then we'd move further and further apart, until one of us won. I remembered overhearing a Spaniard tell his friend in the Bar General:

Cada amor se olvida con otro amor. Recordar el primero amor es amar segunda vez.[1]

But I wasn't capable of creating a love for Rabi'a to replace my love for Kunza. Love is a curse and Kunza was my curse.

As we sat in the Restaurant Puerta del Sol Rabi'a told me, with tears in her eyes, how her mother had died and her father had remarried less than a month later. Her father's new wife had shown her absolutely no affection and she had hated bringing up her brother, who'd been born by Caesarean section. One night her father's new wife went to a wedding. Rabi'a was asleep in her bed. Her father came home drunk and slept with her, apparently unaware of what he was doing. The next day he ordered her to leave Meknes or he'd kill her.

I asked her:

'Did this happen accidentally or was it on purpose? Was that all that happened?'

She held back the tears and seemed more relaxed about it. It had done her good to talk.

---

1. Every love is forgotten with a new love. To recall one's first love is to love for a second time.

9

She's A Good Woman, Though...

I was sitting with the *mukhtar* in the Café Central. He pulled a book from under his *djellaba* and passed it to me:

'This is a wonderful book. A major work of literature.'

It was *Les Misérables* by Victor Hugo, in the Arabic translation by Hafiz Ibrahim. We ordered two milky coffees and I began reading. Because the translation used bits of nineteenth-century Arabic, I had difficulty understanding some of it. There were strange expressions that I found hard to pronounce. However, the *mukhtar* knew the meaning of most of them.

At the bar of the cafe a woman was sitting drinking with a group of Spaniards. She laughed a lot and three of the men were flirting with her. Every now and then she looked across at me. A bright smile, which I duly returned. I wondered what that smile might mean. Women, after all, have their devious ways. The waiter arrived with the two coffees. As he put them down, he said:

'The coffees are on Miss Fatima's account.'

So she wasn't being devious: she was treating us. Presumably she knew the *mukhtar*. I smiled at her again, by way of thanks. Even before the question left my lips, he replied:

'She lives the way she wants with Spaniards. She doesn't mix with Moroccans much. She's a good woman, though...'

The *mukhtar* had this extraordinary ability to recognize people by the sounds of their voices, or even simply by touching them.

Classes hadn't yet begun at the Institute and the class for boarders wasn't receiving students yet. Anyone arriving from the countryside or coming from other towns had to make their own arrangements for food and lodging. In Calle General Ahmed there was a disused grain store that belonged to the Waqf authorities. At this time I had about 1,000 pesetas on me. Hamid arrived and managed to enrol at the Mu'tamid ben 'Abbad school. He continued to get hold of a key to the granary and we moved in.

At night we warmed ourselves by a wood fire that we lit in one of the rooms that served as our bedroom and sitting room combined. We had candles for lighting, and we went out and bought a bottle of Negrita rum to protect ourselves from the freezing cold of the night. We sat and talked about how much we were missing Tangier. On one wall we hung a piece of board that we'd found, and we did our sums on it and tested each other on the various subjects we were studying.

Hamid had met a young girl who'd been living in Tangier, where she'd been roughing it with the down-and-outs. She began joining us in our bachelor quarters when she found occasional generous clients who didn't insist on spending the whole night with her.

She cooked for us and drank with us and contributed to the food kitty. Just because she was young didn't mean that she was cut out for loose living. She didn't have much to say for herself but she was a pleasant, warm-hearted sort of kid. She slept on the floor between us, on a makeshift bed made of cardboard, bits of old cloth and newspaper. She seemed not to mind us taking turns to move up close to her to warm ourselves against her body. But she was obviously less interested in sex than we were. She had a kind of modesty that meant she was passive with us. She was probably like this with everyone who slept with her. Probably all she wanted from us was friendship. But we had never known the simple friendship of men with women—friendship without sex. She was a woman, and we were men, and that was that. We raped her womanliness. Sometimes she cried as she lay between us and that made me feel bad. Hamid, on the other hand, ignored her. The trouble was, we were incapable of seeing her sleep on her own. Apparently her parents had died when she was a child and she'd been brought up by an aunt.

Hamid and I had no way of earning money. My 1,000 pesetas soon ran out, and Hamid had already been broke when he arrived from Tangier. One morning he told me:

'I want you to wear your best clothes today.'

It was Sunday.

'Why?'

'I'll explain in a minute.'

I had a jacket and a pair of trousers that I only wore at weekends—and only then if it wasn't raining. I chose a white shirt and a brightly coloured tie.

'Don't forget to bring your school bag with you and your pen, the one you write your lessons with.'

'But why all this dressing up?'

'I've had a great idea.'

'What's that?'

'There's plenty of unemployed people coming to town from the countryside, looking for work.'

'So what?'

'I'll go out and grab a couple and I'll tell them that you're a personal friend of the pasha's private secretary. Then you write a letter for each of them, saying: "The bearer of this letter is looking for work, and hopes that you are in a position to oblige."'

'Is that all?'

'Yes.'

'And supposing they catch us...?'

'Who?'

'The police. Or our victims.'

'We'll just deny everything. Have you forgotten how to play dumb? What happened to your days in Tangier?'

'And how am I supposed to deny the evidence of my own writing?'

'Just write in a different handwriting to your normal one... They're hardly going to call in the experts for a case like this.'

'If this all goes wrong, I'm blaming you.'

'The hell you are... You swallow your tongue!'

He set off in search of likely victims. I made my way to the Café Etoile, wearing my best clothes. I sat and read for a while—*The Nymphs of the Valley* by Gibran Khalil Gibran. When

Hamid finally appeared, he was accompanied by a couple of peasants. They were extremely respectful to me as we exchanged greetings. I felt embarrassed, so I asked them to sit down. By the looks of them they were very poor. Hamid sat next to me and explained what they wanted. I wasn't used to this sort of scam. I drank my black coffee while they ordered a pot of green tea. Hamid had no scruples when it came to getting money, even though in this kind of situation the victims were inevitably going to be from the same class as ourselves.

'As far as I'm concerned, everyone and everything is fair game. You and I have to find the money to complete our studies. If they want to get money, they're going to have to go out and steal too...'

This was Hamid's comment once he'd sent our victims on their way. He'd charged them 100 pesetas for the letter-writing and all they got for their money was the following: 'I, the undersigned [...], being a Moroccan citizen from the village of [...], am looking for work. I hope that you can help me to find employment. Allah smiles on his servants when they go to the aid of their brothers.'

They hadn't been able to sign their names, so I dribbled some ink from my pen onto a sheet of paper and got them to sign with their thumbprints.

The following Sunday we were hanging out in Calle Real. We had no money to buy anything at the café. All we had was some cigarettes, which we smoked one at a time, taking turns, a drag each. Hamid was dawdling behind, looking in shop windows, so I stopped and looked in another shop while I waited for him.

Suddenly I heard him yelling. Our two victims had appeared. One of them had already grabbed Hamid and the other had spotted me and was heading my way, shouting and yelling. I ran off as fast as I could. Ducking down an alley, I found myself at the back door of the big university mosque. It occurred to me that I might be able to escape by hiding in there, so I ran straight in, without stopping to take my shoes off. In the ablution area I slipped, but managed to regain my balance. I turned and looked behind me. The son of a bitch was right there, taking off his shoes. No chance of hiding there! Unlike him, I kept my shoes on. It was the hour for midday prayers. I hurdled over the backs of the men at prayer and ran right through the middle. They reacted angrily. I went flying out of the main door, and found myself in the square of Souq el Kubaybat.

I yelled at the silly bastards:

'Go back to your prayers. Nothing's happened!'

Stupid damn sheep, they didn't listen! They all started running after me. Some of the store holders in Souq el Kubaybat started running too, so that by now I had a whole gang breathing down my neck. It was a case of 'run rabbit run'. I headed for Aïn Shaqa and stopped at the wall overlooking the sea. Just behind me I could see my pursuers stopping too, out of breath and looking completely stupid. I tried to catch my breath as I leaned against the wall and watched them. There were fewer of them now. They were intent on revenge, but they also looked nervous—a fear of the unknown. They started coming towards me again, more slowly this time; then they stopped to rest for a moment. And then they started running again, so I started running too. They stopped and talked together briefly, and then came closer. I stopped, coughing and out of breath, and leaned against the wall. The sea breeze seemed to revive me and in the end I managed to give them the slip.

In the evening I went back to the granary. There I found Hamid with Saida looking after him. His left eye was swollen and he had a plaster on his nose. Saida had the air of a nurse in a convent—like one of the Sisters of Mercy, nursing a wounded soldier somewhere back in the Middle Ages. Hamid and I looked at each other for a moment. Then we burst into raucous, hysterical laughter. He said:

'You're lucky, you got away from the bastard chasing you. He was a lot stronger and a lot meaner than his pal. He came back and started knocking me about. His friend tried to break it up. Some passers-by stepped in and it was only thanks to them that I didn't end up being hauled off to the police station. If they catch you, they'll knock hell out of you.'

There was a light knock at the door. The knock of a timid person, I thought. Hamid opened the door. It was Fatima. She asked if I was in. I wondered what she wanted. I said hello and we smiled at each other. She was looking agitated, though. She was wearing ordinary clothes and no make-up, so her face looked different to how I'd seen her at the Café Central. I introduced her to Hamid and asked her to come in.

'Not today, thank you. I wanted to talk to you.'

I excused myself from Hamid and went off with her. He

watched us go, showing no interest.

'Don't you remember I invited you for supper at my house? You haven't been to the Café Central for days. I was expecting to see you there and I've been asking the waiter where you were.'

'These last few days I've been going straight back from the Institute to the granary to get my homework done.'

She lived in Calle Real. A small flat: one room, a kitchen and a toilet. The decor was neat and simple. On the walls hung some framed pictures, their edges trimmed with red ribbon. Supper was cooking—a mouth-watering smell of meat and spices that made me even hungrier than I was before. She'd left the lights on when she came to get me from the granary. There was a bottle of vermouth and some lemon juice. I reckoned that Hamid was probably cursing women by now.

'Would you like a drink?'

We drank a toast. Then she put down her glass, as if suddenly remembering something.

I studied the photos on the walls. There were some of her on her own and another with two Spaniards. There was a photo of an elderly man and woman. Her parents, presumably. And a picture of her with a child.

She came back.

'This is my daughter, Salwa.'

A shy, smiling child.

'Give the gentleman a kiss.'

Salwa's lips planted a warm kiss on my cheek. I kissed her lightly on the head. I hate the kind of low-life characters who kiss children on or near the mouth after they've been kissing prostitutes on the mouth, and other places besides. As Hamid says, there's no such thing as a God-fearing man, and there's no such thing as a clean pussy either.

'She's 7. She's at primary school.'

I smiled at the child and sat her next to me.

'This is the gentleman who'll be teaching you when you come back from school.'

She brought me the child's exercise books and I flicked through them.

'Excellent work.'

'I want her to study so that she can be a doctor or a teacher when she grows up. That's right, isn't it, Salwa? I don't want her to end up like me. The only schooling I ever had was three years at the Spanish convent. They taught me needlework and dress-making when I should have been learning to read and write.'

This was the first time I'd met a Moroccan child with the name of Salwa. She smiled and seemed lost in her thoughts. As we ate supper, Fatima was tearing off pieces of meat and either putting them in Salwa's mouth or handing them to me. We clinked glasses. Fatima was a bit high on her happiness. After supper, she said she had to take Salwa to a neighbour who would be looking after her for the night.

'Why don't you let her sleep with you?'

'I get back late at night and I don't wake up early. She has to be up at 7 so as to get to school by 8.'

I asked Fatima where she was from.

'I was born in Larache but my parents are from Ithnain Sidi el Yamani. My mother died and my father went back to the village. Since then he's remarried and now he spends his time farming our land.'

The fact that we'd been drinking created a kind of intimacy between us. She wasn't the brazen sort; she flirted with me a bit, in the same way as she did at the Café Central. Shy in her movements and softly spoken. When we ran out of conversation, she seemed overwhelmed by a kind of sadness, but it was a sweet sadness, so I let her be and amused myself by looking at the pictures on the walls. When the sadness passed I shared in her happiness.

On my way back, I ran into the *mukhtar* Haddad. He was making his way down the street on his own. I stopped him. He reached out and felt me, and then transferred his hand onto my arm, sliding it down till he gripped my hand:

'Ah, Choukri. I've been looking for you. I was hoping to find you at the Café Central. Shall we go there and read?'

He'd probably recognized me by my smell. He was carrying a book—*Laila Who is Sick in Iraq*—by Zaki Mubarak.

'I don't have the price of a drink,' I said. 'All I've got is cigarettes.'

He put his arm into mine and we went off together to the hostel at the Religious Institute, intending to borrow money from a bedouin student who was staying there. However, as we entered the front hallway, he turned left and began to feel his way down the corridor. He stopped at the third door and knocked. No answer. The door wasn't locked. He opened it and went in. When he came out again, he cocked his head to left and right, as if he was seeing with his ears. He had his hand through the slit in his *djellaba*, and was obviously carrying something under the garment.

'What's that?'

'Sh! It's an oil stove. We're going to sell it. I hope we don't run into him on the way out.'

'Who?'

'The owner of the stove, of course. I give him Arabic lessons.'

I left him to wait for me, near one of the arches of Souq el Kubaybat, and I called round to see Salahami at his restaurant. I found him holding up a live chicken by one wing.

'O mighty cockerel! Your hour of destiny has arrived. Dictated not by my hand, but by the hand of those whose wish is to eat you. Verily I have no choice. Your time has run out and verily I mourn for you. After today, no more will you dream of making love and jumping on the hens as they scratch around for food. What a head you have—so high and mighty! You look at the sky more than you look at the ground. Farewell, O mighty one, O delicate one, O handsome one!'

Then he cut its throat with a razor and tossed it to the ground, where it thrashed about in the dust. Its eyeballs were bulging from its head as it leapt and jerked about. It was Salahami's custom to make a ritual address to every chicken that he butchered. He never killed hens. In his opinion, hens were only fit for laying eggs. He claimed that their meat was fatty and tasteless, because they wore themselves out producing so many offspring and worrying about them. That was his opinion. Also, he always killed his chickens with a razor instead of a knife because he didn't want them to feel pain: a chicken isn't a violin, he'd say, it has a soul. I sold him the oil stove for 30 pesetas. When he inquired whether it was stolen, I swore that it had belonged to a student friend of mine who needed the cash to buy a schoolbook. The *mukhtar* and I split the money between us. Before we went on to the Café Central he asked if I would mind making a detour down the road where his sweetheart lived—the 'Virgin'. As we came to the door of her house, he stopped and sighed. Then we carried on. I wondered whether he had smelt her presence. The *mukhtar* was the kind of man who still believed in the old principles of platonic love. This frail lover was to die during an operation for a weak heart, some time in 1974.

'Does she love you?'

'I don't know.'

'Does she know that you love her?'

'I think she does, but it doesn't worry me whether she knows or not.'

'Have you ever spoken to her?'

'Not just the two of us on our own. When she's with her friends at the Institute, we say hello, and sometimes we talk a bit.'

We found a seat in the Café Central and I set about reading him *Laila Who is Sick in Iraq*. He sighed as I read and carefully explained the words I didn't know.

At the Institute I found that my name was on the list of those who had been admitted to the boarders' class. It was Saturday and term would be starting on the following Monday. Fatima was delighted for me and kissed me on both cheeks. It was Sunday when I arrived, and she was making herself pretty to begin her day around the bars.

'Mind you don't ever stop visiting me... And make sure you keep up the lessons with my Salwa. I'm relying on you.'

'Your Salwa is my Salwa.'

She slipped 20 pesetas into my hand and smiled. I didn't refuse the money. After all, she had a job, whereas I was facing the prospect of being more or less broke for the whole school year until the time came for the summer holidays and my return to Tangier. I gave Salwa her lesson for the day and took her out for a while. I bought her some chocolate with the money her mother had given me. We went for a walk and played for a while in the park. Then I took her back to Lilafatina, her childminder.

When I got back, I found Hamid reading a book while Saida was frying some fish. On the trunk stood a bottle of wine and two half-empty glasses. Saida must have bought the wine because Hamid was broke.

Being admitted to the boarders' class was not exactly a privilege —although the beds were decent and we had food from the elementary school canteen, the fact of having to obey the harsh rules laid down for boarders made me as restless as a caged animal. I was in a room where the majority of boarders were middle-class kids from towns in the north. I thought of asking the headmaster to transfer me to another room with poor country people like myself, but who was I to ask for something like that? They'd ask for an explanation and I'd probably get into trouble.

They were all bunk beds. Mine was on top and the bed below was occupied by a boy from Qasr el Kebir. He didn't mix with the other boys. His only interest in life seemed to be arithmetic. In other subjects, he did his homework, but he never bothered going over it again. He was scruffily dressed and only shaved once a week. Wherever he went, he took an exercise book with him, full of algebra and geometry exercises. He'd write on the floor of the room, on the toilet doors, and anywhere the chalk would work. On the wall next to the bed he wrote with a lead pencil. He kept a candle in his pocket, and it was not unusual for him to light it several times during the night to solve one of his algebra problems, writing on the floor.

He never slept right through the night because he needed to get up and go to the toilet several times—first soon after he got into bed and then again several times before morning. He usually skipped breakfast in the Institute dining hall, but I'd heard that he was from a well-to-do family, so perhaps he had his own food. He regularly had nightmares, which kept me awakes at night. He used to talk in his sleep, too. Short, meaningless sentences. Sometimes he seemed to be answering someone who was talking to him. He'd reply with a shrug of his shoulders, or a tight-lipped smile, and then he'd stop. I reckoned that this boy was somehow different from the others in the dormitory, even if he was from the same social class.

One day all these boys would end up as smart, well-dressed young men who shaved every day. Maybe even twice a day if they had a date with a girl in the evening. At the weekend, they'd all crowd round the mirror in the washroom to shave. I couldn't be bothered to wait for my turn, so I filled a bucket with water, leaned over it and used the reflection as a shaving mirror. One of them asked me:

'How did you learn to shave like that without cutting yourself?'

'I practised on my pubic hair. I nicked myself plenty of times, but that's how I learned not to cut my face.'

The headmaster used to come and inspect us in the canteen and in the dormitories. He had studied in Cairo. We respected him because he was willing to help us when we had problems. He never complained when people asked him questions, and I asked more questions than most. Once I met him in the street and asked him to explain a verse by Abu el 'Ala el Ma'arri: 'People were born to live, but certain people wrongly thought that they were born to die.'

He explained the poem and told me about the life of the poet, the times he lived in and his philosophy of life. Sometimes when I saw him in or around the Institute, he'd be muttering to himself, and I reckoned he was probably reciting classical poetry or verses from the Koran.

I didn't forget Mr Abdullah's cafe. Hamid tended not to go there. He preferred sitting with Salahami in his restaurant, eating whatever there was to eat and smoking *kif* with him. Or he'd visit Muwanfarir in his barber's shop, drinking wine with him in the evening, or during the day if it was a school holiday. Usually the only clients that Muwanfarir got were newcomers to the town, and they rarely came back a second time because the man was an alcoholic. His hands shook as he shaved his clients. In fact the only local people who ever came back to him were drunks like himself.

Most of the pupils travelled away on days when there was no school. On one particular Sunday morning, which was cold and cloudy, I'd had a cup of tea and then gone to give Salwa her lesson. Seven or eight customers were in the café playing cards. As I came in, Mr Abdullah turned to a stout man and pointed me out to him:

'There's one of them...'

He sat me next to the man at their table. His name was apparently Bandir and he was missing most of his teeth. Mr Abdullah continued talking to him as he walked across to stand by the stove:

'This young man's a student, so he should be able to solve your problem.'

Bandir asked me, in a not particularly friendly way:

'Are you really a student?'

'Yes. Why—do you have a problem?'

'Mr Abdullah can explain better than me.'

Mr Abdullah prepared a tea for me and then sat down:

'This gentleman is a beggar. He wants to get married and his bride-to-be is a beggar like himself. The trouble is, the registrar says that before he can marry them, he needs something that this gentleman does not have. In other words, money. He's a travelling storyteller. She sells incense. Why don't *you* write them a marriage contract, and we can be witnesses, and Allah will bless this union. The marriage of a beggar to a beggar!'

I knew of no law that said that I couldn't do what I was about to do. And anyway, poverty is above the law. I said:

'And why not, in the name of Allah?'

The storyteller went out and then returned, bringing a woman who was veiled and wearing a gown. She had a squint in her left eye and was carrying a large basket full of merchandise. Mr Abdullah brought us into a room. We sat on a mat, since that was all the furniture there was. He laid out two sheets of white paper for me, and then went out and left me to draw up the contract. This I did. In addition, I duly recorded the extent of their worldly goods. I gave one copy to the man and handed the other to Mr Abdullah. He brought us a second round of tea and invoked a blessing on the proceedings. We both raised our hands. I began reciting a prayer and Mr Abdullah ended it off with an Amen. Then I murmured in a low voice an Arabic poem by Mahyar ed Dulaimi that I had once learnt:

'Among all the people of her tribe, Umm Said had eyes only for me, and she came asking after me.'

The man handed me a few crumpled banknotes. I declined them, saying:

'Never. I did it as a favour.'

He was insistent:

'Take it. It's just a small token... for luck.'

Mr Abdullah added:

'Please, accept this blessing from him.'

When the couple had left, Mr Abdullah told me:

'That was the best good turn you'll ever do. There's a great future in store for you, God willing.'

'Amen.'

I went to visit Fatima. I was surprised to find her looking sad.

She smiled as she let me in, but her eyes were moist and her hand was cold and limp. Before I could ask what was making her sad, she told me:

'Salwa must be sick. She won't eat anything. She's got a temperature.'

'Children's illnesses pass quickly. She'll be alright.'

Salwa was asleep in her mother's bed. On the small table next to her stood a half-drunk glass of orange juice.

'Tomorrow I'll take her to a doctor I know,' I said.

The look on her face was as if she'd never known a day's happiness in her life. As if the grief was piling up inside her. At that time on a Sunday I usually found her dressed up in her best, but on that particular day it was obvious there'd be no perfume, no dressing-up and no going out. Salwa's sickness took priority over everything.

She asked what I wanted to drink.

'Tea or coffee?'

I declined the offer gently. I promised I'd come back in the evening. Out in the street, I felt as if all her sadness had somehow transferred onto me. I found myself walking in the municipal park. The sky was overcast. There was no one about. I remembered Salwa playing among the Spanish children there, and I recalled their mothers sitting and knitting and chatting and warning their children when their games got too boisterous. I thought back to Salwa's mother drinking at the bar of the Café Central. Big drops of rain began to fall and a sudden breeze blew up. I left the park at a run and headed back towards the granary. When I got there, I was surprised to find the place stacked with dozens of sacks of cement.

'What's all this for?'

'It's for building the mosque which Mohamed el Khamis is going to dedicate in town. The contractor's agreed to pay me 25 pesetas a day if I let him use the granary to store it till the mosque is finished. Manna from heaven! Sometimes the Lord throws the likes of us into stormy seas but he doesn't let us drown.'

'Where's Saida?'

'Gone to the market.'

He was flicking through a book about the history of the Phoenicians in North Africa. He said:

'Did you know that it was the Phoenicians who first taught the North Africans how to read and write?'

'Before them, people used to worship stones—the Druids and so on. But the roots of the Berber language are Semitic, or so I've heard.'

I sat down. On the box-cum-table stood a half-bottle of wine. Hamid poured two glasses.

'The headmaster at the Institute has said that I'll be allowed to attend lessons, but not to take exams. If I'm not up to it, I'll have to go back to Tangier, to be a pimp or a thief or a criminal again. Anything could happen if I don't make it with my studies. Mind you, you're no better off than me... You'd have to go back to working in one of the cafés, or in the port...'

He was right. I didn't have magic fingers like his, for stealing from other people's pockets.

We downed the last of our drinks.

'Fatima's upset because her daughter's sick.'

'Prostitutes tend to worry about their children more than married women do.'

Saida came in carrying a large bag of shopping. She had a young woman with her whom she introduced:

'This is Aisha.'

Hamid sat her cheerfully on the box. He was generally polite to women in their presence, even though he said terrible things about them behind their backs. Saida lit a cigarette and busied herself at the stove in the corner, preparing lunch. Hamid and I were sizing up the new arrival.

She accepted a cigarette from me. Hamid lit it and then he asked:

'Where are you from?'

'Qasr el Kebir.'

'So we're neighbours. I'm from Azila.'

I gave him 10 pesetas to buy a bottle of wine and he asked me:

'Why don't you stay and have lunch with us?'

'I can't. They mark absences in the class register. If I'm absent too often, they'll take away my grant. I'll be back after lunch.'

I found *mukhtar* Haddad walking on his own under the arches of Souq el Kubaybat. I stood in his path, blocking his way. This time he greeted me by name without even needing to touch me. It was as if he could recognize me even from my smell. Under one arm he had a copy of André Gide's *La Symphonie Pastorale*, in Hassan Sadiq's 1978 translation. He told me:

'This is a novel by a French author. They tell me it's one of the best things he ever wrote. If you like, we could read it together this evening.'

I agreed readily. Then he asked me to go with him to the street where his beloved Virgin lived. I saw three girls coming down the street towards us. They were looking over at us and laughing. The *mukhtar*'s body was electric with excitement. He gripped my arm tightly:

'There she is—that's her, coming with her friends.'

'There are three of them.'

'The most beautiful one is the short one...? The one with rosy cheeks... Am I right?'

'You are.'

'Pretend you haven't noticed them. Just carry on as if nothing's happened. Don't even look at them.'

When they'd gone, whispering among themselves, he told me:

'I'm supposed to start giving one of them Arabic lessons tomorrow.'

'Which one?'

'The brown-haired one.'

He left me near the Institute and carried on picking his way down the streets that he knew so well. At about 4 o'clock I went back to Fatima's. All the worry made her look thinner than usual. Salwa was sitting up in bed. Her cheeks looked flushed. Her mother sat next to her, smiling at her. I patted the child's cheek and stroked her hair. The way that Salwa looked at me was as if she was seeing me for the first time. She'd probably missed me. She looked somehow worried too. Fatima poured two glasses of Martini and handed one to me. On the radio Abd el Wahab was singing: 'From her eyes came the call of love.' I don't think I ever saw Fatima angry, but she was the kind of person who could be bright and happy one minute, and then get horribly depressed the next, over the slightest thing.

I found Hamid on his own. An old RCA radio, with the sound of flamenco coming from it. A light bulb hanging on the wall bathed the room in brightness. The radio had been a present from Muwanfarir the barber, since he hadn't used it for years. Hamid had invented a system of stealing electricity from the street outside. The problem was that he could only use it at night. He showed me how to disconnect the wire and pull it back into the granary first thing in the morning or before going to bed at night.

'What about a ladder to disconnect the wire?'

He pointed to some boxes:

'Those are my ladder.'

'Where are Aisha and Saida?'

'They're out on the job. They'll be back this evening with some food. Why didn't you come back after lunch?'

'I had a nap, then I went over to Fatima's. Her daughter seems to be getting better now.'

I sat down:

'I'll have to get back to the Institute tonight. Like I told you, they keep a register of absences.'

'Screw the register! Aisha's going to spend the night with us. She's all yours.'

Aisha and Saida returned, bringing some food and two bottles of wine. So to hell with class registers! There were plenty of ways of earning a living in Tangier. I was beginning to get the hang of reading and writing and I no longer needed other people to read books and letters for me. I thought back to what life had been like with Fawziya, and the easy friendship of Hamid, in the Hotel El Qasabah, and the thought of all this left me with a mixed sense of both happiness and sadness. Saida and Aisha came back with the shopping and put it down. Hamid picked up a book and opened it.

'What are you reading?'

'A chapter on the history of the Assyrians and Babylonians.'

'What's the point of filling your head with stuff like that? It's no use for anything.'

'I don't agree. Everything that happens now is grafted onto what came before. History matters, whether we like it or not.'

Hamid poured wine into the only two glasses we had. He and Saida drank from one glass, and Aisha and I from the other. Then there was a knock at the door. Hamid got up from the bed and made his way barefoot across the floor. He opened the door to find an elderly man standing there, shabbily dressed. Hamid helped him to load four of the sacks of cement onto a little handcart. I thought:

'Not a bad way of earning some money fast—but we'll be in big trouble when the contractor finds out...'

Hamid switched on the radio. There was the voice of Asmahan, singing 'Enjoy your youth in Vienna'.

I said:

'If they find out we've been stealing electricity, they'll throw us out on our necks.'

'No problem. We just look for another place. After all, this is hardly a palace, is it? So we've nothing to lose.'

Hamid's always ready to start a new life—start all over again. He never sticks to anything. The way he sees it, everything in life is fragile anyway and liable to fall apart from one minute to the next.

I finished reading *La Symphonie Pastorale* with the *mukhtar* in two sittings. As we sat in the Café Central, he sighed and said:

'I don't know why fate is always so cruel to good people and brings good things to bad people. What did poor Gertrude do to deserve what happened to her in the book?'

'I think that the "shepherd" was wrong to fall in love with her. He was the one who ruined her. If he'd left her to his son Jacques, she wouldn't have succumbed to despair and committed suicide.'

'This is one of the things about men of religion. Sometimes they defile people who are pure. But then again, Gertrude died as a woman and didn't end her life as an animal.'

Hamid joined us at the Institute, but he didn't take the lessons very seriously. He'd made friends with one particular student, who was encouraging him to skip classes. He had one foot in the Institute and one foot in Tangier, so that if he failed with reading and writing, he could just go back to picking people's pockets. As for the sacks of cement that he was systematically stealing every night, he blew the money on drink and hanging out. He didn't split the proceeds fifty-fifty with me—he just gave me what he felt like. He was the boss of the granary, so he could do what he liked. He could even bring other girls back to the granary and sleep with them right under Saida's nose. He bought himself new clothes, a Parker pen, and a leather wallet which he was always flashing in front of the teachers. He spent his days hanging round the bars. He bought some smart clothes for Aisha and Saida, trying to outdo their better-paying clients. Spanish perfume too. They were beginning to look like top-class call girls.

We were in the middle of exams when a letter arrived for me, written in Spanish. It came from the TB hospital in Tetuan. The handwriting was elegant. It looked like the kind of writing they taught in convents. 'The writer of this letter sends greetings and urges you to visit your mother as soon as you can.'

On the final day of the exams I went to see Fatima. I told her that I needed to make a trip. She insisted on giving me 100 pesetas, which she tucked into my jacket pocket.

'Don't worry—everything'll turn out fine. Today you can travel like a teacher or a lawyer and forget that you're poor.'

Salwa was not there at the time.

Hamid invited me for supper and suggested that I spend that night at the granary. I found Saida and Aisha in their prettiest clothes. The smell of their perfume was overpowering... Hamid had bought some secondhand furniture and decorated the walls with pin-ups that he'd cut out of magazines. He'd made a little bookshelf from a plank of wood and some bricks. I asked him:

'How are things working out with your Spanish contractor?'

'A wonderful man. The best thing about him is that he doesn't keep a close eye on things. As they say, he's the bread of Allah! He still seems to like me, so I don't think he suspects anything.'

'You've been overdoing it a bit, though, with the fancy clothes and the furniture for the granary...'

'Don't you think he's stealing too? From the funds for building the mosque...'

'Could be.'

'So stop worrying, then.'

Saida and Aisha looked even prettier than usual and Hamid seemed unusually friendly. Probably it just felt that way because I was about to leave them for ten days.

10

Family News

I met a vegetable seller I'd known in Trancats and he told me that Tafersiti was now living in Bourj el Af'a. I hadn't seen him for the best part of six years. I found him in the Café Saniya playing cards and he took me back to his place.

As we went down the street, several houses had prostitutes standing in the doorways. Some of them were peering out at the passers-by, while others kept out of sight. They looked very sexy and inviting. There were men hanging around outside, both young and old, watching the girls. Occasionally one would go up and inquire how much it would cost, and then he'd either go in or move on to one of the others.

We went into the Bar Rebertito and ordered a couple of sherries. The bar still had some of its former splendour—down to the stuffed bulls' heads hanging on the walls. This was the first time I'd ever actually been into the place. I only knew it from when I was a kid. In those days I used to grab the left-over drinks off the tables outside. I'd drink whatever was in the glasses, whether lemonade or wine, and then I'd go round picking up dog-ends off the floor. The bar was now used by white-collar workers, Moroccan small businessmen and the remnants of the Spanish military presence in the city. Tafersiti worked during the summer selling fridges with a Spaniard. For the rest of the year he dealt in wholesale fruit and vegetables, like we used to in the old days. I asked him about his one-time girlfriend, Latifa.

'Oh, she got married. She's got three kids now. I had a lot of girlfriends after her, but they all ended up wanting to get married.'

'Didn't you ever think of marrying one of them?'

'Never.'

'Why not?'

'It's not right for a man to marry a prostitute.'

'Why's that?'

'You can't go making children with a woman who sells herself.'

'Why not? What's so difficult about that?'

'They'll have problems later in life when they find out that their mother was a prostitute.'

His big dream was to marry a woman who wasn't living off immoral earnings, partly so that his kids wouldn't grow up with problems and partly so that she wouldn't be unfaithful to him. As far as he was concerned, if a women was a prostitute, it was a dead cert she'd end up going with someone else.

My questions seemed to disturb him, so he changed the subject:

'You're OK—you've struck lucky.'

'How do you mean?'

'You've been to school. You seem to think about things a lot.'

'You could study too, if you wanted. You could go to evening classes. They're starting them all over the place.'

'I don't think so—luck's passed me by.'

I didn't want to argue with him, for fear of putting him in a bad mood. As far as I was concerned, I'd end up going crazy if I didn't study.

We finished our drinks and went back to his place for lunch. In the evening he came with me to Sidi Talha, where we used to live. He knocked at the door of a small tin hut. Out came Arhimo. He told her:

'This is your brother Mohamed.'

She smiled shyly and there were tears in her eyes. I put my case down and we hugged each other. It was as if I smelt on her the scent of my whole family, both those who had died and those who were still living. The tears were running down her cheeks. I was crying too—but inside myself. A young boy came out. I reckoned he must be my brother Abdelaziz. His feet were bare, his clothes were worn and shabby, and he was pale and thin. Arhimo smiled through her tears as she told me:

'This is your brother Abdelaziz.'

She lifted him up for a kiss. He'd been 1 year old when I left Oran in 1951. Now he was 7. He still hadn't learnt how to smile or laugh. His face was a picture of timidity. Tafersiti asked me to call round at his place later and then he left us. In the second of the two rooms, Arhimo picked up a little girl for me to hold:

'And this is your sister Malika. She's 2. You didn't know about her?'

'No.'

'Mother's a bit better now. She isn't coughing up so much blood. Father's gone to Sebta to sell some honey.'

'Honey?'

'Yes. He makes it out of sugar and leftover honeycombs, and sells it to the Spaniards. He usually stays there for two or three days, so he should be back this evening.'

When I came back in the evening, I found our neighbour Abdelhamid sitting on a chair in front of his hut. He was obviously waiting for me. He ushered me in. In one corner I saw my suitcase. It looked as if it had taken a battering.

'Your father's a damn fool. We country folk are harder on each other than we are with outsiders. He wanted to burn it. It was your sister Arhimo who stopped him—she found him breaking it up.'

One of the two big frames in the case had its glass broken and the mount attached to it was split. The most important thing was that my exam certificate hadn't been damaged. Our neighbour begged me to stay the night at his place, but I tucked my bag under my arm and left.

On my way back to Tafersiti's I went into the bar in the Saniya brothel and had two glasses of Terry cognac. I smoked one cigarette after another, aggressively, wondering how I was ever going to rid my life of my father's presence.

I found Zahra preparing supper. She welcomed me with open arms. I gave no indication of the turmoil inside me. Tafersiti had gone out to buy bread. I was suddenly seized with the idea of buying a knife and going back to stab my father—or working out some way of getting my brothers and sisters out of the hut and setting fire to it while he was still asleep inside.

Tafersiti returned. He came and sat next to me, and as we talked I told him:

'My mother told me that my father hit my grandfather, and kicked him, and insulted him in her presence, when they lived in the Rif. If you ask me, his side of the family are all criminals, bastards and madmen.'

Zahra said:

'Allah protect us!'

Tafersiti said:

'He'll live to regret it.'

'I don't give a shit for his regrets.'

He opened a bottle of wine and said:

'Come on, let's drown our sorrows.'

He took Zahra aside for a moment and they whispered together. She put on her *djellaba* and went out, smiling. I asked Tafersiti about Aziza and her son Abdeslam.

'She died last year. TB. It was the wine and the *kif* that killed her. Abdeslam copped a two-year sentence three months ago. They charged him with various robberies.'

'And Sebtaoui?'

'He had to get out of town fast. He went to Sebta. The pair of them had gone and robbed the Jewish shop in Souq el Trancats. They cleaned out the safe one night.'

Zahra came back. She had a slim girl with her, whom Tafersiti welcomed warmly.

'Lovely to see you, Mina. We haven't seen you in ages.'

I shook hands with her and she gave me a friendly smile.

The following morning Zahra brought me up breakfast. I saw that there was 150 pesetas on the tray.

'Mohamed left this for you.'

'And Mina?'

'She's working for a Spanish family. She lives with them. She's got no family here in Tetuan—she's from Sama.'

I left 50 pesetas for her to give to Mina. She shook her head and handed the money back to me:

'You need the money more than her. Anyway, she's a friend.'

She was insistent, so I took the money. Maybe she wasn't a prostitute after all. As I went out, Zahra said:

'So we'll expect you for lunch. Try to be here by about 1.'

11

A Hospital Visit

There were four beds in the ward. In the bed next to my mother's was a young woman who appeared to be bed-ridden. Her sickness gave her a certain beauty and she had a good colour in her cheeks. I placed a parcel of fruit on the little table and kissed my mother on the head; then I sat on the small white stool next to her bed.

My mother said:

'This is Miss Ghaliya, who wrote asking you to come.'

I thanked Miss Ghaliya and we smiled at each other. She blushed, and coughed several times in embarrassment. I imagined that she must have been taught by nuns, judging by the neatness of her handwriting. I told my mother about having seen my brothers and sisters. I didn't tell her what had happened with my father. She told me that they didn't allow children to visit relatives at the hospital, and so the only visit she'd had was from Arhimo, because she was older than the others. Sometimes our neighbour Abdel-hamid had visited her too, together with his wife. My father, on the other hand, hadn't come to visit her once.

Ghaliya coughed repeatedly and painfully. Her face became red and flustered and she took a spoonful of something from a small bottle. An open window was letting the cold into the room. My mother said:

'They leave it open even when it's snowing, so as to keep fresh air coming in. We keep warm by using plenty of blankets.'

I explained that I'd passed my elementary certificate and she was obviously delighted, although there were tears in her eyes and she began coughing. Ghaliya was coughing too. I wondered whether I'd reminded her of her schooldays.

'Did you see your father?'

'Yes. He's pleased I'm doing so well in my studies.'

I knew that my sister Arhimo would eventually tell her everything that had happened between my father and me, but that would be another day.

A woman came in and sat on the edge of her bed. My mother told her:

'This is my Mohamed.'

She smiled at the woman to make her feel welcome. Then she began coughing again. You could see that she was in pain, from the way her smile was strained, and the way she limited her words and movements. I said:

'The cold must be deadly here at night.'

'They only shut the shutters. The air needs to be kept fresh.'

I promised that I would visit her again before I went back to Larache.

When I went to lunch with Zahra, there were just the two of us. She said:

'He quite often doesn't come home for lunch or supper. He'll be getting drunk and playing cards. He often loses because the men who play with him know his weakness for drink. His trouble is, he doesn't know how to pull out at the right time, when he's on a winning streak.'

It was an unpleasant surprise to discover that I was needing to piss all the time. My cock hurt every time I went to the toilet and any time anything pressed against it. There was pus dripping from it too. It hurt even more when I had a hard-on. The head of my cock was red and it was sore every time it rubbed against my pants. So she *had* been a prostitute after all...

12

The Honey of Human Beauty

It was evening by the time I arrived in Tangier. I took a room at the Hotel La Balata. In the periods between going for a piss, I noticed that there was pus coming from the tip of my cock. I was feeling dizzy and had a slight fever. I didn't feel like going out to eat, so I stayed in and finished reading *Cyrano de Bergerac*. Smoking in confusion and pissing in pain. You dog, Cyrano! Your cock grew so long that it ended up on your face!

By next morning, pissing was even more painful. I was worried by the way my cock was constantly dripping pus. The tip had become redder and even sorer. I described my symptoms to the emergency chemist and he put me on a three-day course of treatment. This was the first time I'd ever seen my cock drip pus, and it was also the first time I'd ever had an injection.

I discovered that Rabi'a had been arrested in a round-up of prostitutes who'd skipped the official medical examination. That cost her one month in prison. Kunza was living in the Hotel Tahiti, in Tariq el Masihiyin. There was an American warship in Tangier harbour and its crew were all over town—in the bars and in the streets, and in the brothels too—the Spanish brothel, the French one and the Jewish one. I ran into three of these sailors (one of whom was a Filippino) in the Inner Souq and offered to take them to the brothel of the beautiful Madame Simone. Anybody who had enough English to say: 'Hello.... Come on... This way...' could have led a whole battalion of them.

There were several girls in the reception area when we arrived —French, Spanish and one Italian. When they sat on a chair, their skirts showed their bare, slender thighs, and the way they stood in their high heels showed their arses to perfection. The honey of human beauty, waiting for someone to taste it. We ordered beers at the small bar in the hallway. One of the girls walked across to us and two others followed. Madame Simone took me aside and said:

'I'll give you 30 out of every 100 pesetas they spend, the usual rate with tourists. Finish your beer and come back after they've gone, or come back tomorrow.'

The sailors gave me 2 dollars apiece as a tip. I had no way of checking how much they were going to spend, but usually brothel madames pay a reasonable percentage, even to non-officials, just to keep sweet with everyone.

Shortly before midnight I left a bar in the port. I saw the drunken Filippino being frogmarched, barefoot, by two US naval police. His white sailor's uniform didn't look so good now. Presumably the police had emptied his pockets and given him a good beating. He'd seemed more level-headed than his friends when I'd taken them to Madame Simone's.

The bitch gave me 100 pesetas. She told me:

'They didn't spend much.'

The price of a session with one of the girls would have been 100 pesetas. My cock had stopped dripping. Not one of them would have me, though. I preferred it at Marie Karkan's. At least there I'd be guaranteed a session. I'd seen plenty of people like myself going in and out. And it would only cost me 50 pesetas. Her girls were Spanish, and they were less snobby about going with Moroccans than Madame Simone's girls.

One of the girls was Christo Valina. I knew her from when I'd sold her smuggled cigarettes the year before. As I stood at the small bar, Marie Karkan was talking with a client. I ordered a glass of sherry. Christo Valina was sitting at the bar, smoking and thumbing through a fashion mag. I offered to buy her a drink. She was happy to accept, in a voice that was definitely sexy. She was drinking Cinzano. We clinked glasses. I lit her cigarette for her and she said:

'I haven't seen you round the Inner Souq for a while. Don't you sell cigarettes any more?'

'These days I'm studying in Larache.'

'Well, you're better off doing that...'

We ordered two more drinks and went to her room. She put a dark violet-coloured pastille into a bowl, and dissolved it in warm water so as to wash herself. She gave me a bar of scented soap for me to do the same. She poured *eau de cologne* onto pieces of cotton wool. She gave me one of them and we wiped the fronts of our bodies. Sitting naked on the edge of the bed, we drank from our glasses, and kissed, and made love, and talked a little about the way Tangier was going fast downhill. She was born in Tangier, and had subsequently discovered that her mother had also been a prostitute. Her sister had been similarly engaged for a while before getting married to a young Moroccan who was a smuggler. We made love again and the scent of her armpits mingled with the scent of her perfume. Her breasts were plump and I could see the image of my face reflected in her eyes.

13

Sweet Distance

Before I could even knock on the door of the granary, a young girl from the house over the road called across. She was playing hopscotch with her friend, on white chalk squares on the ground. She said:

'If you're looking for your friend, they came and threw him out.'

Then she carried on with her game. She spoke to her friend in Spanish and the friend replied in Spanish too:

'Shall I jump now?'

'No.'

'Shall I jump now?'

When they'd finished one round, I asked:

'What do you mean, they threw him out?'

'Two policemen came and took him away. They took the black lady and her friend too.'

I booked into a room at the Hotel Maliqa and went out for a stroll. It was 5 o'clock in the afternoon. I went to see the *mukhtar* at his house. He was looking depressed. His mother welcomed me in and offered me tea and black bread with honey and butter. A moment or two later the *mukhtar* said he wanted to go out. Something had obviously happened to upset him. He looked sad in a way that I'd not seen before. When we got to the Café Central, he explained:

'A teacher asked my girl to marry him.'

'Women prefer marriage to love.'

'What's the point of marriage without love?'

'That's the way of women.'

'So a curse on love, then!'

'And a curse on marriage too, because it starts with a yes and ends with a no.'

Salwa's childminder told me that Fatima had gone off to Spain, looking for work. Salwa's grandfather had come and taken her with him to spend her holidays in the country. I presumed that Fatima would be working in a bar or a dance hall somewhere. Hamid had been held at the police station for a couple of days, and when they'd let him out he'd travelled to Asila. Saida and Aisha had disappeared to some other part of the country. I felt horribly lonely. The small world that I had created outside the Institute had been torn apart. The apple was rotten, the orange was split in two, mulberry juice was dripping from two lips, and sweet distance was beginning to create a nostalgic longing.

14

Beauty Revisited

When I passed the entrance exam to go to teacher training college, it felt like I was being born again. I really imagined that I was building an impregnable wall that would shield me from society's contempt, from ignorance and from life's miseries. That was stupid of me. As it turned out, my happiness was outweighed by bad luck.

My father's only interest in my exam pass was the fact that he'd be getting money out of my monthly grant. He'd started complaining about having to provide food for me and about letting me stay in his rat-infested shack—at least until I collected my first grant cheque. He was the kind of man who worshipped money more than he worshipped God, but he wouldn't lift a finger to earn it—he expected others to earn it for him.

All my dormant hatred for him was rekindled. Relations between us had settled into a mutual loathing. I didn't understand why he hated me so much. He never missed a chance of saying bad things about me, whether to my face or behind my back. It had always struck me that he had the face of a criminal—the face of someone who's recently come out of prison after a period of hard labour. How much longer would I let him prey on my mind?

The year was 1960 and it was the summer holidays. The passage of time had put a big gap between me and my old friends in Tetuan. Some of them had long since left the town. I wondered if we'd recognize each other if we ever met again. The only one of our old gang still in town was Tafersiti. He was doing very nicely. He'd more or less cornered the market in fridges and refrigerated vehicles, and had another three businesses going on the side.

We ran into each other fairly often and found that we still had a lot in common. After all, we'd all been suckled at the breast of suffering. He led a strange kind of existence—half the day indulging his sex life, and the other half doing business with the town's traders. Whenever we met, we'd drink a couple of toasts to Independence. Once he took me along to the Via Rosa brothel in Calle Martil. I'd never seen wastefulness on a scale like this. He was pouring bottles of champagne over the feet of the Spanish prostitutes. There were cheers and shrieks of delight: 'Long life to your mother, Mohamed!'

On that occasion I drank the night away, at his expense, until dawn the following morning. I hadn't noticed him leaving. I returned to town on foot. It had been a night to remember and I was still drunk. As I searched for a cigarette in my pocket, I found some crumpled banknotes. It was a few hundred pesetas. Tafersiti must have slipped them into my pocket when I wasn't looking. Or maybe he'd given them to me and I'd forgotten—a black hole.

I used to sit in one of the cafés on the Feddane, smoking *kif* with the customers there. The *kif* was free. I joined in with the card players too, but I didn't gamble. My mother was still slipping me the price of a pack of cigarettes and a glass of tea. Sometimes I ended up not even spending the money because some customer was enjoying my company and offered to treat me. I used to go and read books in the English bookshop, too, and often I'd stay until it closed. Once I offered my services as a tourist guide to a group of middle-aged English couples. They seemed to enjoy my company. I knew enough words of English to show them around and the map of the old city was still imprinted in my memory. They took a photo of me, together with their group, and gave me 100 pesetas, which was enough to last me for a good few days.

My father lost no opportunity to run me down in front of the neighbours and his friends (most of his friends were wounded ex-soldiers from Franco's war, who used to hang out in Plaza Feddane).

'He's just an ignorant bastard like me. Don't tell me he's actually learnt anything! If you ask me, they must have made a mistake in the paperwork when they passed him.'

His resentment against me was endless. If my mother ever protested, he'd beat her and curse her, just as he used to do with us. And the hatred seemed to pursue me even after his death.

His friends went along with whatever he said about me because some of them had sons who earned their living from prostitution—and why shouldn't I be one of them too, so we could all be in the shit together? But there were exceptions. An elderly man stopped me in the street one day:

'Are you the son of Hadu 'Allal el Choukri?'

'Yes.'

'Is it true you're studying to be a teacher?'

'Yes.'

'May Allah be with you! Some people would love to have a son like you, but your father treats you like dirt and goes round speaking badly of you. Your father's the one who's stupid!'

'I know. He was born to hate the whole world. He even hates himself!'

'Allah protect us!'

While I was in Tetuan, a wave of nostalgia came over me—memories of the playgrounds of my childhood, the maze of alleyways, the streets, the outskirts of town. We were young and we got up to all kinds of mischief. I remembered stealing from the orchards up the side of the valley. Sometimes we stripped naked and had masturbation competitions: 'I came first...' I visited Aïn Khabbès and the place where we used to live in Gharsat Baninas. I remembered how we used to fight with sticks and stones. In spring, we celebrated the dew and the sun and the swallows. We danced and we shouted. As I walked about, I heard an invisible cockerel crowing from some place nearby. I remembered a rainbow, and how we rode donkeys, and hung onto the backs of lorries as they drove off. The fig tree was still there, tall and green. There were creepers climbing up it, twining round the branches and hiding some of its beauty. Things are always more beautiful when you look back on them. That childhood magic stays with us all our lives.

I'm writing some of the chapters of this book in 1990. During the summer of last year, I had a visit from a Japanese friend, Nutahara, who was in Tangier together with his wife Suku. He was translating *For Bread Alone* into Japanese. Having completed three pages, he had stopped:

'I decided that if I wanted to do a really good translation, I ought to go and take a look at the places where the things in the book happened...'

We set off from Tetuan on the way back to Tangier. The water cistern was the first thing we came to. He took lots of photos of it, from various angles. When he finished, he smiled and said:

'In your book you described this cistern and everything around it as if it was very beautiful. But it's not. What's more, there's nothing to suggest that it was beautiful even in those days.'

I told him:

'That's the purpose of art—to make life beautiful even when it's ugly. In my mind's eye I still see this water tank as beautiful, and that's the way I'm always going to remember it. Even if it was really only a muddy puddle. What's more, when I wrote the description, I was a long way away from it, in time and space.'

I now returned to the water cistern again. The midday heat was scorching. I stood on top of the tank gazing at the house where we had lived in the early 1940s. A house of daily conflicts between my parents. A house that was poor, but had its moments of beauty. Today it was radiant with white paint and a new door. When we lived there, the paint was dull and peeling and the place was falling apart. I remembered trying to patch it up several times with planks that were even older than the house itself.

A woman came out of the house. She was getting on a bit. Her broad bosom was sagging but she had a clear, open country face. A young woman appeared behind her, surrounded by barefoot kids.

'My family used to live here.'

'What was your mother's name?'

'Maimouna.'

'We moved in when you left. I know your mother. I haven't seen her for ages. Where do your folks live today?'

'In Sidi Talha. Barrio San Antonio.'

'How is your poor mother?'

'Not too bad.'

'I'll visit her one day, if Allah wills. Give her my best regards.'

'I shall.'

I had no loose change to give the kids and nothing to offer the woman either. I made my excuses and left. I walked down Tariq el Nakhil, looking back on my memories with a mixture of happiness and sadness. The Instituto Baylar still stood there, large and looming.

I read for a while, but after that I couldn't think of anything to do. If I'd been in Tangier I wouldn't have felt so totally bored. In Tangier even if you find yourself completely penniless and depressed, something interesting or enjoyable always seems to come along. Solitude there is free and wild, and tastes of wild berries; here it was constrained and tasted like shit. I took a stroll to the La Pergola cabaret, which was advertising tango-dancing (Carlos Gardel and Concha Bakir), flamenco, Las Cublas (folk singers) and gypsy dancing. There was the house where the young Italian woman used to live, with the bin in front of her door from which I used to scavenge fag ends stained with the red of her lipstick. I remembered how smoking them used to bring a kind of sexual pleasure. I went for a walk in the park. I didn't even have the price of a cup of tea in the Café Maghara. Hadi Jouini was singing 'Under the jasmine tree in the night'. My mother's business was usually sluggish in the middle of the month, so it wasn't always possible for her to give me money. A scented breeze was blowing.

I found that it soothed my spirit to be in the middle of all this greenery, where young lovers come so that they can be alone. There were only a few small goldfish left in the pond. Somebody told me that the drunks who slept in the park had caught all the rest and grilled and eaten them. The ducks in the park had disappeared completely. There was a monkey in a cage, with children teasing it, and a smiling photographer offering to take pictures of the courting couples. I looked at these Moroccan lovers, fascinated with the idea of freedom. It was the period when they were plucking up courage and beginning to come out from their hiding places, out into the streets, under trees, in cinemas, in European clothing and wearing ties. A strange picture of men and women in mismatched colours, with the women stumbling along in high-heel shoes. Innocent vanity and harmless coquettry. The age of the lover hadn't yet come.

I walked round Trancats, and the Upper Souq, and Gharsat Baninas, and the ghetto (the Jewish quarter) at least once a day. The sight of the traffic, the sounds of people working, and the hubbub of the traders and shopkeepers in these streets, made the day a little less boring. But on the other hand I had an alarming thought that one day I might end up stuck right back there in Tetuan, working in those same streets. I'd had enough of all that shit and humiliation when I was a kid.

I was sleeping in one room together with my brothers and sisters, and my parents slept in the other. My father and I weren't talking. So as to avoid seeing him, I used to get back at about midnight. As soon as he heard me coming in, he'd start his muttering and cursing. Mostly it was directed at me. My mother would certainly have been asleep. Since she never answered him, I assumed that he was talking to her as if she was awake, as if she could hear him. Then, eventually, when he got tired of cursing her for the pigs that she had borne him, he fell asleep and began to snore. He and I were both as stubborn as each other. He disapproved of me as a son, and I disapproved of him as a father. Our rows were getting steadily worse as the days went by. One thing was certain—he was interested in nobody but himself. He had no time for people, animals or things unless there was something in it for him.

By the beginning of September I was just wishing that this lousy summer would be over as soon as possible, so that I could sink back into autumn, and then winter, and the cosy warmth of memories...

I didn't often come back to the hut of disaster and ill omen during the day, but on this particular day I did. I was tired and hungry. My brother Abdelaziz was selling sesame cake and sweets to the kids in the street from on top of a box, which he pretended was a grocer's shop. The boy was a born businessman. He was busy counting out his takings in front of us, and he checked them through several times. He was proud of what he'd earned and he challenged his sisters to earn anything like it. If he'd dared, he would have challenged our layabout father too.

I found Habiba listening attentively as my mother and my sister Arhimo talked with her. My other sister, Malika, was fast asleep on my mother's shoulder, with her head close to mother's head. My mother's closeness with Habiba was a continuation of her friendship with Habiba's mother. Habiba's mother had also had a hard time with a cruel, dissolute husband, but she'd fought with him until she was eventually defeated by death. The father had forced Habiba, his only daughter, to marry a middle-aged friend of his, a cattle dealer, when she was barely 17. The man divorced her just over a year later because she hadn't borne him a child. Her father and her aunt were horrible to her, and she had nobody she could turn to for protection.

They stuck her in a mental hospital, because she started breaking things around the house and she'd taken to tearing her clothes. In the hospital she used to go into wild dancing fits, until in the end she'd either pass out or the doctors would give her an injection. After a few months, she was discharged, to return to normal life.

In the summer holidays she met a young man on the beach at Martil. He was on holiday with his family. He married her in Tetuan and she went to live with him in Rabat. He was working as an odd-job man and she had four children with him. But he was cruel to her, beating her viciously, until, in the end, she walked out on him, leaving him with the four children. He divorced her and she went to Sebta, taking her madness with her. In Sebta she started her dancing fits again and she used to hang around the working-class areas, getting drunk, flirting with the men and making fun of the women. She had no place to live, so she used to sleep with any of the tramps who'd give her shelter for the night in the Principe. Sometimes she'd make a wreath of flowers and put it on her head, and then she'd walk along dragging four clattering metal plates behind her, each tied on a separate piece of string. These metal plates symbolized the four children that she'd left in Rabat with her 'barbaric' husband, as she called him. When she was in one of her lucid phases, she got on well with people and they used to give her food and clothes. But her disorderly behaviour finally got so out of hand that the authorities moved her to Tetuan and put her into the Hospital for Nervous Disorders, in an attempt to cure her of her hysterical fits.

Once again she left hospital to begin a normal life, in an attempt to leave all that behind her. She started taking care of herself and bought smarter clothes, in which she'd parade, like a child, through the streets of the city. Her father owned shops and flats.She lived in one of them, on the ground floor, and above her lived her widowed, childless aunt. The father decided to give them both a monthly allowance to live on, but it was a pittance. Eventually Habiba married for a third time, after having spent years wandering the streets. And in the seventh month of this marriage she died of cholera while she and her husband were expecting their first child.

I found that I enjoyed being in Habiba's presence as she discussed her worries about her husband and her children in Rabat with my mother. After a while, Arhimo went out, together with Fatima, her best friend from across the street, and my mother began busying herself at the stove in the yard of the hut. Malika was still fast asleep. Habiba asked if I'd like to go to her house for supper. The thought of this cheered me up a bit. She lived in the Maliqa quarter of town. Before she went, she slipped a crumpled 1,000-franc note into my hand.

'Buy something to drink. I need to go out for a while. Wait for me in front of the cinema.'

My mother was busy with the cooking. She never questioned me about my comings and goings. Either I slept in the hut or I didn't. This was a long-established understanding between us. She watched me going out as she was in the process of putting something in a saucepan.

'I'm going out.'

She nodded and didn't say a word. She wasn't the sort to give me meaningful looks. Her dark eyes had an eternal sadness in them. She always showed me more affection than she did to my brothers and sisters. Maybe this was because I was the eldest and had been saved from starvation by a miracle; maybe it was because I'd been born in the Rif and spoke with her in the language of her family; and maybe it was also because I was living away from home. My brothers and sisters, who were born in Tetuan, didn't speak dialect and they didn't understand much either. They weren't at all interested in learning it. My mother used to speak to them in Rif dialect, but they always replied in Arabic. As far as possible they always tried to hide their origins. They thought that people from the Rif were backward. I knew a lot of people who thought like that, young and old alike.

I stopped off in the Barrio Maliqa to have a couple of glasses of wine in a Spanish wine shop, and I bought a bottle. Habiba had described her flat to me. It was simple and neat and reminded me of Fatima's house in Larache. A bedsit, belonging to a single woman who took pride in keeping her place clean and polishing the furniture. The room was lovingly decorated. On the wall hung a picture of herself as a girl with her father in Bab et Toute, as well as a photo of herself in traditional wedding dress and a large framed portrait of her mother. There were a couple of dolls on top of a low wardrobe, a ticking wall clock as well as a cuckoo clock, a bedside table with a small lamp, a marble-topped table with a mirror on it and various bits of make-up, and a vase containing a single red rose and some white flowers.

We ate our fish supper, drank the wine and afterwards smoked a cigarette. Then we began talking about life's problems. When we got tired of that, we agreed that the only way that people find out the truth about themselves and about others is through misfortunes and disasters. Habiba had let down her hair. It had been in plaits when she was at our hut. She seemed more beautiful now. Her movements were measured and graceful, her voice was gentle, her conversation was unhurried and happy, and she had a tranquil, almost sleepy look.

As I talked to her about my studies in Larache and my life in Tangier, her mind occasionally seemed to wander. I was happy that she'd invited me to sleep at her place. It meant I didn't have to listen to my father spewing out his garbage all night in the hut of ill omen. She begged me to sleep in her bed and she would sleep on the couch, but I insisted on sleeping on the couch. I went to bed fully clothed. Darkness settled. She put the light out and there was silence. The evening wasn't the best I'd ever enjoyed, but it had been good.

Habiba turned over in bed several times. She couldn't get to sleep. Lust was beginning to get the better of me. For more than two months I hadn't touched a woman's thigh or breast. I was missing the pleasures of sex, although masturbation had its own pleasures (and its advantages too, because it doesn't tie you down, and it's free of the inconveniences of long-lasting relationships and venereal diseases). Had her invitation to me been just an act of friendship? Was it because she wanted company or had it been desire? It was desire—of that I was certain, judging from the way she'd looked at me. But I didn't know what her dormant madness might have in store for me. I didn't want to be the one responsible for setting her off on more crazy dancing.

A part of me was getting excited and pushing me towards her. In my Tangier days I'd more than once found myself waking up in a hotel, or in a friend's house, and not knowing the woman who was sleeping with me. Or sometimes I'd find that she'd left while I was still asleep, without my seeing her go, and leaving me with nothing but the memory of my cock inside her. It was usually drunkenness or a chance encounter of the night that brought us together, but Habiba wasn't a chance encounter, and we weren't drunk either.

I suspected that I would be taking advantage of her kindness if it turned out that she didn't want me. Why couldn't I just relax and enjoy the night—enjoy the sublime silence and the closeness? Why does desire have to spoil everything that's beautiful? I got up, walking quietly like a thief, and slipped into bed with her, still fully clothed. She was sleeping curled up in the foetal position. Her hair was hanging over her face. All of a sudden, she stretched out, as if relaxing, and then returned to her previous position. She whispered, as if in a dream, or as if she was extremely tired:

'Leave me alone. I'm asleep.'

'I love you.'

'Spare me the jokes for tonight...'

It was stupid of me, she was right. But I carried on with my play-acting. I tried kissing her and touching her, because in a way I wanted to be sure of her rejection. She just lay there, inert, making it obvious she wasn't interested. She knew what she didn't want. I'd obviously misread the situation. Suddenly I felt her body shudder and stiffen, and something warm and wet on my trousers. She'd pissed herself. Had she pissed in her sleep or was she awake? Did she have a pissing madness as well as a dancing madness? In a brothel in Tangier once I'd slept with Pissing Laila, but she hadn't pissed like Habiba had pissed.

I backed off before I stirred up some other madness in her. I took my trousers off and lay face down on the couch. She was crying. Was she purging herself of my insult or was she trying some kind of come-on? Either way, I wasn't in the mood for playing games. Some women don't soften towards a man unless they cry, but I haven't the patience for games like that. What had made her piss? Had it been fear or a muscular spasm? Either way, I'd thought that Habiba was a human fruit, ripe and ready to be picked, or lying rotten on the ground. But I'd made a mistake. For me, at least, the fruit was not yet ripe.

15

A Bird of Happiness

My mother bought me a jacket, two shirts and a pair of trousers for the start of term at teacher training college. When I told her what had happened with Habiba, she said:

'I'm sure you know what's best for you.'

The demon of literature had begun to take possession of me, and I was discovering I was more interested in literature than in educational psychology and educational planning. My greatest interest was the Arabic language. We had a good Arabic literature teacher. He'd write a text on the blackboard, and after he'd explained what it meant, he'd take it apart to show us its grammatical structure. He was a practising Moslem, but he had a good sense of humour too—in his left hand he held the world, and in his right the hereafter. On Fridays, in one of the small mosques, he'd lead the people in prayer and preach a sermon. In the evening he'd go out for a night on the town, in Rincón or Sebta. I went with him sometimes, in his old car. He used to keep a mousetrap under the back seat. He was convinced that he had mice living in his car. It must have been a clever mouse, because it only ate part of the food he put there.

The teacher who taught us educational theory and psychology caught me reading *Les Misérables* and threw me out, shouting:

'This is supposed to be a classroom, not a reading room!'

I began to frequent the Café Continental. It had a relaxed air about it and you could see from the faces of its clientele that most of them were fairly well-off. The 49,000 francs which I'd received as my grant was a considerable amount in the 1960s. I gave part of it to my mother and kept the rest for myself. I divided my time between reading in Arabic and reading in Spanish, and having a good time round the bars. The Bar Rebertito, with its walls decorated with bulls' heads, was the best-looking bar of all of them. I enjoyed the songs I heard over the sound system in the Continental. Two songs that I never tired of listening to were Nat King Cole's 'Unforgettable' and 'Bésame Mucho' by Antonio Matshin.

There was one particularly striking man in the café. He was elegant and seemed to command the respect of the rest of the clientele. He generally had a group of people around him, all as chic and prosperous-looking as himself. I asked someone:

'Who's that man?'

'You really don't know? He's the writer Mohamed el Sabbagh.'

'What does he write?'

'Poetry. Free verse, mostly.'

I bought some of his books: *The Thirst of the Wounded*, *The Paralysis of the Hunting Dog*, *The Tree of Fire*, *The Moon and I* (the last two translated into Spanish) and some shorter books. I read them in two days flat. I told myself that if people respected those who wrote like that, then I would write like that too—or even better. So writing did have its advantages... I had no idea that writers might actually be seen in public places and might speak to ordinary people, the way that Mohamed el Sabbagh did in the café. I always imagined that writers were either very private people or they were dead. I settled down and wrote three pages of text. I called my piece of nonsense 'The Garden of Shame'.

I began to watch Mohamed el Sabbagh. Eventually, one day, I saw him sitting on his own, drinking his usual instant coffee. I went over to him, nervously:

'Are you Mohamed el Sabbagh?'

'Yes.'

'I've read your books and I like them a lot. I want to be a writer too. This is the first thing I've written. I wonder, would you mind taking a look at it and telling me what you think of it?'

He tucked my three pages into his pocket. I said goodbye and left the café so he wouldn't feel I was pressurizing him.

At midday the café was almost empty. He was in the habit of calling in for a coffee before going on to work in the public library. He gave me back my writing the following day, saying:

'Your language is not bad at all. Carry on writing. Try to be disciplined and read a lot.'

I took to drinking coffee with him while I told him bits and pieces about my life in Tangier, my studies in Larache and my course at the teacher training college. He gave me suggestions for good poetry to read in Arabic and Spanish: Gustavo Adolfo Bécquer, the brothers Antonio and Manuel Machado, Pablo Neruda, César Vallejo, Gabriel Mistral and Rafael Alberti... And I discovered for myself the romantic purity of the women poets: Rosalía de Castro, Emily Dickinson (translated into Spanish), Susanna Marsh, Juana de Ibarbourou and Alfonsina Storni. Some of them had written more than one book, and there was I still struggling to write a single decent sentence. A story from Morocco, by Ahmed Abdeslam el Baqali, was the first thing I'd read by a Moroccan writer.

A newspaper published a short prose piece of mine, 'The Stream of My Love', with a picture. I was wildly happy and I got drunk to celebrate my hidden literary talents. I bought several copies of the paper and distributed them among my fellow students to make sure they realized I was now an important person. I was impressed: a son of the shanty town and the human dunghill writes literature and they publish him! So as to increase the sense of my own self-importance, I treated myself to a good jacket and a pair of trousers, plus a selection of bow ties and a fake gold wrist chain. Vanity and inflated self-opinion got the better of me and I abandoned the popular cafés in the Feddane, Trancats and the Barrio Maliqa, and began to frequent the patio of the Hotel Nacional and a dance hall called the 'Marvel'. I began to hang out at the Café Continental and the Bar Labara. I shaved once and sometimes twice a day, which wasn't too good for my skin. I began to use scent, to the extent of carrying round a small scent bottle in my pocket. Ibn el Baraka and Ashir el Fi'ran were chic, were civilized and were progressive... I'd shed my old skin and grown a new one. And what about inspiration...? Oh yes! A very necessary thing, inspiration. Imagine it—me, a son of the gutter, seeking inspiration..!

One day I followed a young brunette. I knew where she lived, and her family background. I began to shadow her every time I saw her, or I'd watch her from in front of her house or in front of her aunt's house. A friend of the daughter of a Moroccan political leader. She was called Halima and was a neighbour of Habiba and a friend of my sister Arhimo. She was illiterate but she was brunette and pretty. Maybe she'd inspire me to writing gypsy poems, but she was too passive to inspire me to anything greater. I was used to women made of sterner stuff.

Habiba gave me a key to her flat, so I came and went as I pleased. Sometimes she didn't spend the night at her place. More than once I saw her in a car, or walking down the street in the company of someone I didn't know, in the area of Nazhat Jadid! She would pretend not to have seen me. Fair enough—that was her business. She vanished and didn't reappear until the following Tuesday. She had traces of a blue bruise over her left eye. A heavy blow. Someone was giving her a hard time. My sister Arhimo contracted pulmonary TB. My father and my brother Abdelaziz were also coughing violently. A total epidemic in our family. Malika and I were the only ones unaffected. My mother had recovered but she was still under medical supervision at home. My father was the only one being treated without supervision.

Habiba disappeared again, this time for a couple of days. I decided to move to the Hotel Black Jewel. It was a small family hotel run by two Spaniards, Rosario and Carrion, who were brother and sister. Twenty thousand francs a month, one small room and three meals a day. I presumed that Habiba was having an unhappy love affair with someone.

I visited Arhimo and Abdelaziz in hospital. Arhimo burst out crying—a woman had died in her room, so she'd got it into her head that anyone who fell ill would die. By this time our mother was pretty much bed-ridden.

I accompanied Mohamed el Sabbagh to his flat in the old part of town. The ambience of a person devoted to his art. Grapes, apples and pears in a large metal bowl; a subdued light that deepened the effect of the poetic silence. Chopin: 'The Nights of Majorca', and reading letters by Mikhail Nu'imah. I came out from his house wishing that I had a refuge like that. He went through my writings and corrected them, using words that were finely sculpted, transparent—but he was clay of one kind and I was clay of another. He didn't have to eat the garbage of the rich. He didn't have lice like me. His ankles weren't all sore and bleeding. I wasn't capable of writing about the milk of small birds, and touches of angelic beauty, and grapes of dew, and the paralysis of hunting dogs, and the songs of nightingales...

I called on Habiba to give her back the key to her flat. She looked pale, tired and desperate. Her voice sounded tense and hoarse:

'Why did you go? What upset you?'

She looked as if she'd been crying.

'I didn't want to be a bother to you.'

'You weren't a bother at all.'

On the *taifor* stood two empty beer bottles and a pack of Virginia cigarettes. A new worry was starting to get her down. She seemed on the edge of collapse. Even her aunt was refusing to see her, saying that Habiba was shameless. Her aunt was married to the foreman at a local garage. Habiba didn't have any other women friends. I suggested going to get something we could drink together. Her face lit up. I wanted to see her looking happier. Her sadness reminded me of Fatima in Larache when her daughter Salwa had fallen sick. Salwa and a winter's day in an empty park. Salwa whom I had not seen since.

I stopped Habiba reaching for her purse. There was a hint of a smile, and then the smile opened out and her face became young and beautiful again. We would have supper together. Lamb with artichoke and chickpeas. A cool, invigorating breeze was blowing and it was drizzling.

I went into a Spanish wine shop for a glass of sherry. Two middle-aged Spaniards were chatting about the art of bullfighting and how it had deteriorated into commercialism. They sighed over José Barandas, and Marcial Lalanda (Chiquillo) the Brave, and Francisco Peralta, and Joselito El Gallo, and Manuel Mejías Rapela (Bienvenida), and Juan Luis de Larousa (a fascist who'd been killed in Barcelona at the start of the Spanish Civil War) and Manolete El Azim. When the discussion started getting heated, the owner of the wine shop stepped in to referee and calm things down.

I had a second glass and went out to buy a bottle of white wine. I thought about Habiba as I walked back: it was probably best for her not to go falling in love again, in case she ended up going back to her crazy dancing in the hospital and in the streets of Sebta. But then again, maybe she found it a good way of relaxing and letting off steam in this rootless life of hers. Her last divorce had robbed her of most of her self-respect and she'd never really had the chance to develop beyond the age of 25. She'd had her four children like a rabbit: twins first, and the other two in quick succession. In order to manage the housework, she used to tie the kids' legs to the end of the bed, the settee or the table, to keep them apart so they wouldn't scratch each other or snatch pieces of biscuit from each other. She'd never had the chance to live a decent life. It had been bad luck all the way and she'd had to steal the few moments of happiness that she'd had.

A delicious smell of cooking wafted from the kitchen and pervaded the flat. The room had a happy, bustling air. Her words began to wipe away the dust of sorrow from her face. We drank toasts to this and that, and there was a warm feeling between us. She was smiling, as if she was really enjoying herself. She had prepared meat with artichoke and chickpeas, which was her favourite dish. I ate it and it was delicious. She called it the 'First Vizier'.

She looked at me tenderly and said:

'I haven't found anyone else who understands me the way you do.'

'We shouldn't trust too much in happiness. It's a fleeting thing, disappearing the moment we try and catch hold of it. It's like a beautiful little bird that lands on the edge of a balcony. No sooner do we approach it than it flies away. Do you believe that this little bird is going to land on your shoulder, or mine, and sing for us?'

'I understand what you're saying.'

'So maybe this is happiness, then: instead of the bird landing on your shoulder to sing, it stays on the edge of the balcony and sings there.'

She agreed with me and, sighing happily, seemed more relaxed.

'You're right.'

I was also comforting myself with the thought that my life was no more wonderful than hers.

16

The Dreamers

It was a fresh, breezy morning as I left Habiba's house. I felt as light as a feather, as if I was walking on air. She was still asleep. The door clicked shut behind me. My trousers were still slightly damp.

I ordered breakfast in the Café General Yazid. There was an old wind-up His Master's Voice gramophone in one corner, dating from the 1940s. The records they used to play were mainly Om Kaltoum, Asmahan, Abdel Wahab and Farid el Atrache. They kept the gramophone as a kind of memento of things past, a testimony to their memories and the culture of earlier days.

I decided to wait until my mother went off to sell her second-hand clothes in Bab et Toute and my father went, as usual, to the Feddane, complete with more cock-and-bull stories about his so-called bravery in Franco's war. His friends in the Feddane, like himself, had been deserters in Franco's war. His stories were all lies. The only time my father was ever brave was in his war with us, and he began to lose that war once we started growing up.

When he could no longer trash us, he would sometimes beat our mother, to the point of drawing blood or giving her a black eye, or two. One day he'd beaten her so hard that it had exhausted him. At that point he'd lifted the metal pot in which he boiled the sugar needed for making the honey that he sold in Sebta. If it hadn't been for my mother's screams alerting the neighbours, he would have tipped the contents over her head. When the neighbours came, I grabbed the pestle from the mortar and threatened to smash his head with it if he started his craziness again. He rushed round to the man next door and burst out crying:

'The bastard threatened to kill me. He threatened me with the mortar. I should have strangled him when he was little, that would have sorted him out!'

I had a sudden vision of my brother Abdelqader's blood spurting out when my father had wrung his neck. However, that was the last time he hit my mother. From then on, he confined himself to abusing her and cursing us.

I found Arhimo coughing feverishly. When her coughing stopped, she cooed like a dove. My mother had left her some orange juice, saying it would do her good. I washed my trousers, shaved and then went and bought one of Abdelaziz's little cakes. When I told him I hoped business would be good that day, he answered jokingly:

'Well, you're the first customer I've had today, so let's hope you bring me luck.'

He kissed my small coin and put it in his pocket. We smiled at each other and I left. As I was setting off down the road, I heard Fatima, our hunchbacked neighbour, calling after me. She said good morning and I greeted her in return. Then she disappeared. She had a pretty wretched time with her handicap. She used to cheer herself up reading cheap paperback romances, and writing love letters for her women friends who didn't know how to write such things. She was the public scribe, for all the goings-on, big and small, in our street. I realized that all the aspirations and all the wealth of the people who lived in these shacks lay in their dreams. Poor people are the world's true dreamers. In their hovels they dream about making loads of money, and eating big dinners, and holding noisy parties until they pass out with singing and dancing.

I didn't know why I was in such a good mood that morning, especially after what had happened with Habiba. I called round to the English bookshop and read a bit of *Jane Eyre*. Then I went to the Café Feddane. I joined a man playing cards with two others. The stake was the price of a cup of tea. My partner said he'd cover me if I lost. We won, then we lost, and then we won again.

After a while my head was dizzy with the card-playing and the *kif*, so I went to the Café Awmainu (in Rif dialect: 'my brother') in Trancats. I hadn't been there since I came back from Oran in 1951. There I found Comero and Batati. We embraced warmly. Ten years had passed since the day of our memorable fight. We played backgammon for a while, and poured *eau de vie* from a hidden bottle and drank it from a small glass. I tucked myself into a space by the stove to drink my glass. You could see from their faces that they were heavy drinkers. Comero was working as a doorman at the post office. Batati had been working as a co-driver on a lorry until he'd managed to fall off the back. He'd broken his leg, and now he walked with a visible limp. Comero said, jokingly:

'I reckon he fell on purpose, so's he could claim on the insurance and retire on the proceeds. He's so lazy it's unbelievable! Don't you remember what he's like? Have you ever seen him do an honest day's work? His speciality used to be robbing his father, but when his father died he didn't know how to rob anyone else, so he had to get a job.'

I smiled and didn't say anything. I thought: Batati was robbing his father in the café when he took over from him at siesta time, but you were a dab hand at robbing the rest of them!

Comero asked me:

'What about you? What have you been up to? We heard you've been studying in Larache.'

'I passed the entry exam for teacher training college in Tetuan.'

'So you'll be staying with us during your training period?'

'Yes.'

Batati said:

'You're the lucky one out of our gang.'

'How's that?'

'It's a privilege to be allowed to study.'

Then he added:

'Even the best of us is never going to be anything more than a labourer, or a small trader, or going abroad to find work. You've got a guaranteed future now, with the state, and before too long you'll be a teacher.'

'I hear that Tafersiti's a rich man these days.'

'Tafersiti's another matter. You know him better than us. You're two of a kind. He's the sort of person who eats and still worries that he's going to be hungry. The man's a miser. He'd have sold his mother's milk while he was at her breast...'

'But he's happy enough to spend money on himself.'

'Oh, shut up. You don't know the kind of person he is nowadays.'

'I know he spends money on people he thinks are important.'

'See, now you're beginning to understand... Do you realize, he left his father to die in poverty in a shack, while he was living in a smart flat in town? The day he dies, there'll still be hunger on his face.'

Comero said:

'He didn't stay on the dungheap like us, but we haven't sunk as low as he has.'

He added:

'Do you remember Batikha, the one we used to give centimes to, and cinema tickets...? He's got rich too. He lives off exploiting young boys. He's married now, with a family.'

By the fourth glass my head was beginning to spin. I had an alarming thought: maybe Comero was taking his revenge by getting me drunk. The mark of the scar I'd given him was still visible on his left cheek. I made my excuses, saying I had to leave. Comero was perfectly friendly, not seeming to harbour a grudge because of our fight.

'When do we see you next?' he asked.

'I'll be around for the whole year. You'll find me at the café.'

I left them while I could still stand. Another couple of glasses and I'd have been out of my head. It was 7 in the evening. The hut of ill omen would not be asleep for another few hours yet. Trancats was bustling with movement, just as I remembered it from the late 1940s and early 1950s. Probably even busier today. Old faces had disappeared from the shops and new faces had taken their place. Some of the faces were still there, but had grown old. My mother told me which of them weren't there any more, either because they were sick or because they'd died.

Habiba was my saviour that night. I went round to her place again. She welcomed me warmly. She probably understood that I was the best she'd get. Her gentle smile and friendly handshake told me she wasn't angry with me. She probably needed companionship in the same way that I did.

'I hope we can still stay friends,' she said, and smiled.

I nodded in agreement. She was the stronger of the two of us. There was no point in me thinking I was anything better than her. I got the message that she didn't want there to be anything physical between us. The glasses of Mahiya *eau de vie* that I'd drunk were having the same effect on me as Del Mono anis or Terry cognac. They knocked me out. I relaxed to the sound of a female singer on the radio and dozed off. I felt someone put a cover over me. This was just what I needed.

I slept for about two hours. When I woke up, she'd prepared supper and bought us a bottle of white wine. I was feeling a bit dopey, so I splashed my head and face with cold water. Farid el Atrache was singing on the radio: 'O vision of beauty'.

17

Rosario

Rosario liked to boast that she was born in Avilés in Asturias; that she spoke Bable (the local Asturian dialect); that she had a mortal hatred of Franco; and that she'd been married to a republican militant from Gijón who had given his life in the cause of democracy.

Most of the time we—Fermin Vito and myself—sat on our own at one of the four tables in the small restaurant's forecourt area. Sometimes María Rosario would join us, either at his table or at mine, smoking, and sipping a coffee or brandy (or sometimes both together). Fermin Vito was in the habit of boasting about his birthplace too. He was from El Ferrol (which happened to be where Franco was born). By common consent we avoided sharing a table. Once I suggested he might come and sit with me, but he made an elaborate apology and stayed where he was. When I was on my own, Rosario would come and join me. The fact of our sitting together was a kind of secret understanding against Fermin Vito, because Rosario always used to say that he was too smug and self-satisfied for his own good. When he was about, she'd stay at her table on her own, or stay in the kitchen, or bustle about the premises. He was very touchy too, and not at all the friendly sort. She told me as much when she saw him refusing to sit with me.

On this particular night we didn't hear Rosario and her brother

Carrion arguing over their card-playing. Despite the fact that Vito was always getting upset about their shouting, it was as if something was missing in our lives. We could never tell who was cheating whom—Carrion generally protested a lot, but Rosario would shout him down—to cover up her cheating, or so Vito claimed.

When Vito left, I discovered that Rosario had been furious with her granddaughter Cándida. She smoked her cheap cigarettes and drank her vile brandy, and kept popping in and out, with a glass in one hand and a cigarette in the other. Cándida had run away from boarding school at the convent of the Sisters of Charity, in Tangier, three days previously. They were pretty sure that she hadn't left Morocco and they knew she hadn't gone to her mother's in Meknes. In fact, she'd been at her friend Marisa's house in Tangier. Her grandmother had hidden her passport from her:

'She always had a hard time at the hands of her mother and now it's the daughter's turn.'

That's what she'd say to Carrion, but he preferred not to get involved in his sister's arguments. Rosario was getting on a bit. The previous April she'd celebrated her 62nd birthday.

Carrion smoked his cigarettes, which he rolled himself, drank *carajol* and amused himself reading children's comics. When he spoke he had a tendency to mumble, but his sister understood him clearly enough. His nose was broken and scarred, and I wondered whether it had happened in a fall or if someone had hit him. He confined himself to the kitchen, preferring to avoid conversation with the customers.

Rosario had an Andalusian temperament, even though she was from Avilés, and she used all kinds of expressions whose meaning escaped me. She spent a lot of time with Andalusians in Morocco, but most of them had left the country after Independence. One day her granddaughter had come to visit and Rosario found her looking down from the balcony into the street. I heard her shout:

'Close the window, child, or the bull wind will whisk you away...!'

But then came the day when the bull wind really did whisk her away, becaused she escaped over the walls of the Sisters of Charity convent school and her grandmother didn't have the first idea where she'd gone.

I loved it when Rosario got all worked up with Vito, when they argued about the Civil War, or about priests and the Church. She'd argue him into the ground and quote all kinds of things that she'd read. She was lucky, because most of the poor girls of her generation had never been given the chance to study. I always backed her up against Fermin Vito, even when she was wrong. He was in the habit of saying rude things about her behind her back. One evening he was talking about her and he said, in a quiet malicious voice:

'The old witch, her saints have escaped her and gone to heaven.' (By this he meant that she no longer knew anything about anything.) 'At least she's giving us a rest from her usual yelling when she's cheating at cards. I pity that poor devil Carrion—fancy having to spend his whole life in her shadow! She's a heathen and a hypocrite!'

But Rosario had a more evil temper than Fermin, and when she talked about him he really went for the jugular.

'Miser... Opportunist... Hypocrite... He goes to mass on Sunday just to keep in with the Spanish diplomatic corps. He's preparing proper credentials for himself as an insurance for when he goes back to Spain. He needs to look like an upright citizen, so's he can get a better job there. Do you know why he's so keen on Franco? Because he's from the same town, and he thinks he's the best ruler Spain's had since the days of the Catholic kings and queens—Isabella and Ferdinando, and Carlos III. Isn't he stupid...!'

In a sadder tone of voice she told me about her husband, a communist, who'd been executed by the fascists in Tetuan.

'They say that Franco used to order those executions while he was eating his breakfast. Ten per day, so they say. And my husband was one of those bloodstained breakfasts. Do you know how it was that Franco ended up taking over the government? They say it was all the fault of his brother Nicolás. He was to blame for the disaster. Apparently the military law which his colleagues created at the moment of their victory stipulated that Franco was to be *provisional* head of state, but his brother had sent the text to the printers on a top priority military order and he'd crossed out the word "provisional". So that's how Franco ended up staying in power for so long. At the start he'd said jokingly that it was a temporary dictatorship to restore the rule of law in the country, and afterwards he'd retire to the countryside to live in peace. But when things started to go well for him in power, he began saying: "My government will be for life. Spain is a kingdom without a king, but we are monarchists." And in order to cement it in perpetuity, he inevitably had to associate the church in this "god-given" venture, with a view to creating a kind of crusade against the communists. He also had to distance himself from most of the people who'd helped him in his victory or drive them into exile in France, Mexico, Argentina and Russia. He got rid of José Antonio Primo de Rivera,[1] abandoning him to die in Alicante prison so that he'd have no competition in his project to establish fascism in Spain. It was in his power to do an exchange for the socialist leader Largo Caballero, but he preferred to kill him so that he could get rid of both of them. He didn't even trust his own shadow. He wasn't prepared to take risks if a prisoner wasn't any use to him in perpetuating his own power. This hunter of rabbits and boar saw Spain as a kind of military barracks. Do you know why he used to insist on appearing in naval uniform decorated with the insignia of admiral of the fleet? Because he failed the exams for the naval academy in Toledo, that's why. And he attacked the freemasons—that was because they wouldn't let him join. His officer friends used to call him "The Three M's".[2]

So that was how Franco carved out his path to power. And for all that, Vito was not embarrassed to say that the Caudillo was the person responsible for restoring the glory that Spain had lost in 1898.

And in order to restore to Spain some of the glories she once enjoyed in Cuba, Puerto Rico and the Philippines, he set his eyes on Morocco and began drafting simple-minded Moroccans into his army, telling them that it was their mission to make war on those who didn't believe in Allah.'

Rosario continued:

'The ambitions of tyrants have no limits, as everyone knows. I think that Franco was more cunning than his mentor in the

---

1. The founder of the fascist Blue Shirts.

2. *Sin miedo, sin misa, sin mujeres* (or *sin maricones*, as some would have it)—'No fear, No mass and No women/queers'.

dictatorship, Miguel Primo de Rivera. Franco always maintained that he was a monarchist at heart, but royalist Spain had been stuck with the burden of defeat for a whole century, and he believed he'd been sent by heaven to resolve its disunity. Spain wasn't the only country labouring under this delusion. Right after his military coup against the Second Republic, he announced: "We have the honour of being the first state to defend Western civilization from the malign influences of the East." But the worth of this so-called "defence" became clear ten years later, when world opinion had him thrown out of the United Nations Assembly. His government was left totally isolated internationally. A further ten years passed before the United States[1] and the Vatican interceded on his behalf (each for reasons of its own self-interest) and Spain was re-admitted to the UN in 1955. So he finally won the war and was able to spend the rest of his time painting sunken ships.[2]

In his opinion, treason was the best that could be expected from the Popular National Front, which didn't support the army. The PNF frightened him and it didn't trust him either (it was right in this, because he was advancing his own interests on the back of the PNF's sacrifices.) Was it wise, for example, to sentence to death a legionnaire in Morocco on the grounds that he had insulted a superior officer by refusing to eat lentils because he didn't like them? Military victory can only be achieved by discipline and blind obedience from soldiers, even when their generals are mistaken. This was Franco's justification for these kinds of actions. In his opinion political parties were divisive and detracted from patriotism, and from serving one's country. As for the Germans, they saw him as a clerical reactionary, not a real fascist, because he only really believed in running an efficient regime, and in the legitimacy of the revolution of 18 July.'

I wasn't particularly worried about having failed the graduation exam. I realized that I'd knowingly neglected my studies in favour of reading literature, but I did have the consolation of a posting in

---

1. Huge US bases were set up—for instance at Tarragona and Zaragoza—as well as a large amount of economic aid being provided.

2. Franco used to paint as a pastime. His favourite subject was sunken ships.

Tangier. Our neighbour was employed in the education department. He was sure to have notified my father, and my father would have been happy because my failure would have confirmed his opinion that I was basically stupid. Up to the present day I have never felt any particular shame or regret about it.

Abdelaziz and Arhimo soon got better. He went back to school and his little shop, and she returned to her sewing and to looking after the shack. My father never stopped hanging out with his circle of war-veteran friends in Plaza de Feddane even during his illness, but his asthma attacks were beginning to confine him to bed. He suffered from asthma right up to his death in 1979.

I visited my mother in the Souq Bab et Toute. I gave her my monthly housekeeping money and I also gave her a small amount for my father. I knew that he'd spit on such a modest sum, and would curse me as usual, but he wouldn't turn it down or give it away to beggars in the street. It was enough to keep him in snuff and glasses of tea for several weeks in the Feddane. I was more concerned about my mother, not about pleasing him. I kissed her hand. When I said goodbye to her she was crying. She wasn't the sort of person to press me to make family visits. She obviously knew that I'd failed the exam—I could tell by the way she was looking at me—but she didn't say anything. She knew what made me tick—either I'd turn up or I wouldn't, depending on whether the opportunity presented itself. I bought some small presents, for my sister and for Habiba our hunchbacked neighbour.

I saw this brunette in the street. I followed her until she noticed me and stopped in front of a shop window and began eyeing me up and down. She smiled. I resisted the temptation and went to the Bar Rebertito. I thought: crass stupidity. Love's a dirty game. I didn't want a repeat of what had happened to me with Kunza. I remembered the story of Qasem with his Jewish girlfriend Natalie, before he finally went crazy.

It was 3 in the morning. The rain was soaking me as I stood in front of her house. I felt like a dead tree. Her fat, evil dog was barking at me from behind the grille of the garden gate. I raised my eyes to the heavens, feeling dejected, then I closed them. Drops of rain trickled from my eyes. A kind of fever was spurring me on. My mouth was open and my eyes were closed. A failed love. In my memory I recall mostly the darkness and the rain. The dream of her was shattered on that rainy night. All my anger was somehow concentrated in my hands. I found myself pummelling the wall with my bare hands. The rain washed the blood away. At that very moment she was probably at her toilet, and there was I watering the flowers of my thoughts of her in the drenching darkness. Was this the wonder of love? What a load of nonsense! So I raised my voice to the skies. I knew that shadows are a guide for those who lose their way. I became a shadow of myself and I consigned her to eternal oblivion.

I had a few glasses of wine. Then I went to Anita's house in Bab et Toute. She was a prostitute, but that didn't mean she wasn't friendly and welcoming. Her sweet-scented tidiness reminded me of Christo Valina in Tangier. This was the third time I'd been to her place since I'd first met her at the start of the month. I drank two glasses of Del Mono anis at her house.

Cándida arrived from Meknes a short while later with her mother. She refused to return to her Catholic convent. This was the first time I'd had an opportunity to sit with her. We talked about literature and about writing. She struck me as more intelligent than her grandmother had suggested. Rosario blamed her failure at school on the fact that she'd fallen in love with a young man who had emigrated with his family to Cordoba. Her father had also emigrated, fleeing to Canada to escape the fascists, a couple of months before she was born. He wrote a novel about the Spanish Republican fighters in Morocco. We heard about it, but never saw a copy. For us his story had ended ten years previously.

Cándida read a lot. She wrote too—romantic ideas about failure in love, her weariness with life and the bad luck in her family. She was in her early twenties by that time, and life's worries were beginning to give her an air of maturity, but she still had no idea what she was going to do in life. I had bought two bottles of Rioja wine, and a big goose, which Carrion prepared himself because he reckoned he was better than his sister Rosario when it came to cooking poultry. As usual, Carrion withdrew to the kitchen to have supper on his own. This was my last evening with Rosario's family. Fermin Vito didn't come on Sundays, but if he had come he would have gone on strike and stayed in the kitchen, even if we'd all been eating the same meal.

18

From Honey to Ashes

They gave me a post at the mixed school in Hayy Jadid. I was given the preparatory class to teach. The classroom stood next to the playground. It was more or less a wooden shed, and it leaked in the winter and had frogs croaking round it. More than forty pupils per class—less than a quarter were girls. This was education at absolute rock bottom. Pure misery: dirt, hunger and sickness. I picked up a pencil and asked the class:

'What is this?'

With one voice they replied:

'What is this?'

'This is a pencil.'

They replied:

'This is a pencil.'

'And this?'

They replied:

'And this?'

'This is an exercise book.'

They answered:

'This is an exercise book.'

One of the pupils vomited up the remains of some olives. Another one said: 'That's because he eats olives with his father, sir. His father's a drunkard.'

One of the boys kissed one of the girls in class, and she was upset about it. So as to restore her self-respect, I told her to kiss him back. At that she stopped crying.

There was such ignorance around at the start of the '60s. The education system was terrible. Some of the children didn't have pencils or exercise books. They didn't eat regularly either. There was one boy who was particularly idiotic. The others called him 'Tamkhukh'. He always insisted on sitting right in the front row, in any seat that took his fancy. When he wasn't busy hitting people or biting them he kept the class amused. He had big teeth and a mongoloid face. Sometimes he threw paper pellets and chalk at me while I was writing on the blackboard. Once I punished him by rapping him over the knuckles with a ruler, and he glared at me furiously and started to shake. From that moment I tried my best to ignore him. The little beast was enjoying himself. I put in a report to the school office and I made it clear that my work was becoming impossible because of him. The headmaster's response was:

'It's probably better for him to stay with us at school, rather than running round bothering people in the street.'

Tamkhukh had this habit of going and standing right in front of buses, in the middle of the road, so they couldn't get by. The conductor would have to get off and give him money, or something to eat, or make jokes with him before he'd let the bus pass.

In the classroom he used to pretend to be a steam engine, while the rows of pupils behind him were his carriages. 'Chuff, chuff, chuff... Wooh, wooh...' The whole class fell about laughing. He would doze off during lessons or wander in and out as he fancied. Sometimes he went out and didn't come back, and that always put me in a good mood. When he was absent for more than a day I found myself praying that he wouldn't come back at all, but unfortunately he invariably did.

I had a visit from an inspector doing his rounds. I complained about Tamkhkukh's stupid behaviour. He didn't believe that any boy could be that idiotic, so he went up to him and ran his hand gently through his coarse, unkempt hair:

'Why are you making all this trouble at school?'

No sooner had he put his hand on the boy's shoulder than Tamkhukh pounced on it and bit it. The class cackled with laughter until I silenced them with a glare, even though I was struggling to stop laughing myself. This was the last straw—it led to Tamkhukh being expelled from the school, but nobody could stop him wandering round the area and standing in the way of buses and cars and motorbikes. After he'd been thrown out, the other pupils began to feel sorry for him.

In the end I realized that I wasn't cut out for the job. I lacked the necessary patience, but I didn't have a lot of choice. After I'd done my certificate (three years of secondary studies at that time), a committee came to the Abdullah secondary school in Larache and set us an intelligence test. My results put me in the batch that were recommended for termination of their studies because they were too old. Officially my age was 20, but in fact I was 25.

I moved back into the Hotel La Balata. Maybe I was trying to revive memories of Rabi'a and Kunza. I opted for a small room on the roof, with a window that looked out over the sea and the rooftops of the old city. Next door was Tomás El Rojo, in his wooden shack. He lived the life of a spider. He hated Franco to his very soul.

'They used to say that Franco was clever at hunting down "the boars and the rabbits", but that's not true; he was only clever at killing the noblest of the people. It was his hunting friends and their servants who killed the day's catch, and then they'd put them at his feet and he'd have proud photos taken of them. He also used to paint sunken ships, although with no obvious talent. How was it possible for someone who claimed a love of art to have banished Picasso? They say he was also an admirer of Valle-Inclán, but he authorized the killing of Lorca, and he imprisoned Miguel Hernandez until he died, leaving his wife on her own, nursing their son Basil at her breast.'[1] This was what Tomás used to say.

Tomás lived on his own and spent his time either in his hut or on the street. He considered the Spaniards to be a nation of mental defectives—all TV, games of cards, drinking and so on. During the day he sold children's balloons on the Boulevard, and at night he

---

1. A reference to the last poem that the poet wrote in prison, 'Music of the Onion'. It was dedicated to his infant child, after he had received a letter from his wife telling him that the only thing she had to eat was bread and onions.

read the classics—novels in Russian, French, Spanish and English. He drank cheap white wine and smoked Mafrum tobacco. Before going to bed he drank from a bottle of water mixed with lemon juice. He never liked discussing anything in depth—in fact his opinions were confined to a view that nothing was completely bad and nothing was completely good. He didn't like people who analyse things from A to Z, 'from honey to ashes', as he used to say.

I envied him his solitude. He was almost a personification of solitude, a kind of death in life. He was well past 70 by the time I knew him, but luckily he enjoyed good health. He was of the opinion that bullfighting had come to an end with the death of Joselito and Manolete, and he liked Jota El Aragonesa, and the fandango, and the Carlos Gardel tango, and Concha Piquer, despite her sympathies for General Franco. Sometimes we would share a bottle of wine in his dusty hut. Señora Josefina, the owner of the hotel, cleaned the rooms herself, but Tomás would only let her enter his hut to change the bedding. He said she was nosey and a gossip, and he found the smell of her perfume nauseating.

Rabi'a married an officer in the Moroccan army. They got engaged in Tangier. Kunza was dancing in the Kutubiya night club.

The good old days of prostitution in Tangier came to an end. The brothels that were subject to medical supervision were banned years ago. The older and more decrepit prostitutes began to set up shop in backstreet houses and cheap hotels, serving newcomers arriving from the countryside looking for work, and the poor of the city, at lower prices. Some of them gave up prostitution, out of respect for religion and their advancing years, and began working in restaurants, and hotels, and the houses of the *nouveaux riches*. Some of them had moustaches and facial hair, and their teeth were falling out. A few of them who had become rich on their earnings bought houses and land from foreigners who were leaving the country and retired to a life of ease. The others, the younger and better-looking ones, emigrated to countries like Spain, France, Belgium, Holland and Germany.

By the end of the 1960s a new generation of young prostitutes had come of age, emancipated in their dress, their way of talking and their style. As their bodies matured, they arrived in Tangier from all over Morocco, like a horde of locusts. This was the era of the grand hotels and the night clubs, and of drugs[1] and wild sex for Moroccans and foreigners alike.

I was reading every book I could lay my hands on, but I found that literature and psychology interested me most. Wherever I was, I would pull out a pad and write ideas like the following:

> *Café Central: 25.9.1961*
> The woman that I choose to live with for life will only be the right woman for me if she can keep me from going with other women. She must be all women to me. No other woman will have what she has. I'll be able to pick her out from a crowd of other women even in the dark. When the candles go out, each of us will light the other. Even if they cover us with a veil of darkness, I shall see her and she will see me. I have still not found the ideal woman, for she will be a woman of extraordinary light, a woman of transparency.

While I was writing this kind of thing about my ideal woman, I was sleeping with the lowest class of women still to be found in the few remaining brothels in Tangier. There was no soul in my sex at this stage of my life, just physicality, and this was probably my destiny.

I overheard one of these girls saying to her friend:

'Men are always telling me, "You're really beautiful." But I knew that before *they* came along...'

It seemed to me that woman is always a mirror to herself, from her birth to when her life wanes and she becomes feeble. She starts watching and being aware of her body before men do. Masturbation and cheap sex were what saved me from the trap of falling into unrequited love. I discovered early on that I loved the temperament of the prostitute, but I wouldn't have been capable of living with one, because prostitutes believe that men are driven by sex and they spend their time trying to bring their men down to the same level as themselves.

---

1. The hippies who arrived in the city in the 1960s played a big role in spreading the use of all kinds of drugs.

19

Life in the Time of Mistakes

We should dream a little. In fact, do more than dream. Think of the slave chained to his seat, rowing a galley and being flogged till his back bleeds. He tries to stand up, but bullets riddle his flesh before he can even rise from his seat. Or they shoot him down in the night as he flees. Whether he makes a stand or tries to run, the result is the same.

From whom can I take wisdom today? The intelligent ones have either gone mad or they wander the streets, and the ones who would have had the best claim to stay have emigrated and exile shackles them with her heavy chains. The travail of their journey began even before they left. I watched them savouring their last drinks. I saw one of them carrying a handful of his motherland's soil in a small bag, keeping it as a memento. He would probably plant seeds in it during his enforced exile. Roots of mint too, perhaps. And himself driven out by his country's wretchedness. Baynitz used to tell me in Asila that the bad times would be coming. But, I asked him, when had there ever been good times there?

What were those sad melodies that I could hear in the distance? They were music for the departing exiles in the customs sheds, as they crawled towards their destination. Apparently standing, but crawling for all that. The slowness of their progress humiliated them to the core of their being. The shame of their own country was harder on them than the humiliation of their exile. I heard one of them sigh and say: 'I tell you, this night will bury us here.' As if the frightening memories of previous nights were all bundled up in the night of this border crossing. I was used to the sun and the sea. How could I live by a sea without sun? Fog has always been a mystery to us. We wonder whether the sky above our land has lost its colour. The sun smiles at us before it smiles at others—but in other countries they cover her up.

Enough of this nonsense. Learn how to dream of other worlds as the people who live in them dream of them. Don't close yourself in. Often good may come from evil. Their faces may be grim and depressing, but there's no escaping them.

The new bars in the city are having a terrible effect on us. Even the expressions of the people in them are enough to depress you. An air of tension all the time, and fights. And the bar owners are worse than their clients. How I miss Madame Trudie, and Sir Sar, and the Parade. There's nobody going round the bars asking if someone will buy them a drink. The old bars were like 'the tree which covered the whole forest'. They were focal points. But today the new bars are low-life places and their owners are just as bad.

The hour of desire is approaching. It might bring us closer to each other, but how often it takes us apart just when we're wanting to meet and hold each other. Sometimes I feel like a bull in a bullring, coming out of the darkness of the tunnel into the light, thrusting at the air and flailing its hoofs in the sand, a seething mass of energy, as it prepares to do battle with its allotted destiny. This is life in the time of mistakes. I had been polluted by the night of the streets. Even the decent crazies on the streets have disappeared. They've become sensible! They're taking care of their appearance! This isn't some big statement about their lives—it's just surrender. I remember nights dreaming of my faraway home and missing it, nights of missing the streets, and nights of dreaming of distant journeys.

I want to feel that I'm on the move, even if it's only to the outskirts of the city. Give me the earth and dust of a smooth road! All mornings and the evenings await me there.

I was living in Val Fleuri, near my school. I wrote about everything that was wrong with the city. I railed against it. The city's splendours that had once enchanted me were now drowned in hubbub and din. It was a long time since I'd seen a sunrise in the city, and the freshness of the morning dew. I knew that I would enjoy waking up to breezes, or gales, or even floods. It didn't matter. The important thing was the fact of being there. Let's dream a little more—more than just the memories of our childhood, be they happy or wretched.

In Val Fleuri I found that I was beginning to enjoy nights at home instead of nights in the bars. And mornings of mountains and sea rather than mornings on the panting streets and the cafés waiting for their first customers. The only thing that was missing from my nights with their trees and grass was the howling of wolves.

I discovered Heinrich Heine before I discovered Rimbaud, Verlaine, Nerval, Baudelaire, Shelley, Keats and Byron. I knew Heine's 'I love, therefore I live' before I learned about Descartes' 'I think, therefore I am'. Then Sartre came along and planted another concept in me: 'L'enfer c'est les autres'.

I'd always had a close affinity with internal turmoil. Rousseau's *Confessions* taught me how one can gain consolation in the appreciation of the small things that others neglect. But I was getting into a pretty terrible state.

I burned the last of what I had written in Val Fleuri, and went back to my room on the roof of the Hotel La Balata, to sink myself once again into the pollution of the city. I started selling my books, every day, for whatever I could get for them. Then I went and got drunk. I took sick leave, and when I'd sold my books, all I had left was 'New Pages' by Rosalía de Castro and a collection of poems by el Mu'tamid ben 'Abbad.

One night I made public my physical and spiritual bankruptcy. I was in the Brasserie de France. For some reason I was shouting and cursing the Egyptian pharoahs. I threatened the bar owner, saying I'd smash his drinks cabinet if he didn't call the fire brigade—but they came anyway. I had one more drink and then went with them. I heard the bar owner saying to the waiter:

'Poor guy, his books have driven him crazy.'

'I saw him sleeping out one night in a doorway opposite the Bar Monocle. He was using his books as a pillow. May Allah help him!'

20

The Forgotten Ones

There were five beds in the room. At night, in the distance, I could hear the sound of cockerels and barking dogs. I was reading a biography of Van Gogh, and how his life had begun with a dream and ended in despair. Everything was completely quiet. Suddenly there was the sound of shouting. It was getting louder as it approached our room, and whoever it was, they were shouting that there'd been an earthquake. I hadn't noticed anything. I was probably asleep when it happened. A number of patients from the other wards crowded into our room, and needless to say my room-mates woke up one after the other, and all of a sudden everyone was talking about Allah and religion and natural disasters. Yusuf from our room took the lead in the discussion, providing interpretations and explanations. He had memorized the Koran and the *hadith*. Someone told me that he'd been driven crazy by too much reading. He came out with phrases like: 'Allah fears his worshippers when they are too learned' and 'Death is the greatest truth.'

A man by the name of Mansour said:

'A day on earth is better than a thousand days under the earth. Give me a thousand years of life until I get fed up with living!'

Another man, Omar, said:

'That's quite enough of religion! Bring out the bread and water, and the cigarettes.'

Nobody gave him anything, so he covered his face with his blanket and started cursing us for being so mean.

Yusuf said:

'People are sinful like their fathers and forefathers. Pain is fair justice. The happiest man is not necessarily the one who is closest to Allah, and the most miserable man is not necessarily the one who is furthest from Allah.'

There was one young boy who was shouting all the time:

'Cut off my hands. Here they are, cut them off!'

Yusuf said:

'Passing time is death. They visit the living with the self-same flowers with which they visit the dead. The flowers of happiness are the same as the flowers of grief. People's hearts have become like butterflies flitting around flowers that have withered.'

When we went out into the grassy yard, Abraham began singing us his song:

'On earth and in the sky, long live love.
In my country and in exile, long live love.
In prisons and in places of worship, long live love.
In huts and in palaces, long live love.
In alleys and in graveyards, long live love.
In houses and in hospitals, long live love.
In peace and in war, long live love.'

Mansour was sitting near me, enjoying the smell of a flower with childlike simplicity.

'It's not easy for a man to go mad; and it's difficult to become wise enough not to go mad.'

Yusuf said:

'People's understanding is a burden and their bodies are their donkeys. Once I saw a porter load his donkey cart with sack after sack, until the cart collapsed and the donkey collapsed too. He was trying to cut down on how many times he had to return to load up. A step is a step, but who is able to take that step? Everyone is scared of an imaginary chasm that they have before them. We fall before we walk. How tall are the trees, but how short are people! Truly the secret of life lies in the secret of growth.'

After we'd had our fill of sunshine and fresh air and the clear blue sky, we went back to our room.

Abraham came in. He wouldn't leave us alone until one of us gave him something to eat. I gave him a chunk of bread and some olives. He was always hungry, no matter how much you gave him. Bread and olives was one of my favourite foods too. Abraham swallowed more than he chewed. He hardly chewed at all. He was tall and sturdily built, and at night they'd take it in turns to go and have sex with him. He never complained unless the rape was accompanied by a beating. And what they did afterwards was even more revolting: they'd bring the hospital dog and get it to lick his backside, where it was streaked with blood. Mansour asked him:

'What's your girlfriend's name, Abraham?'

Most of the time he talked about her without needing to be asked.

'Esther.'

'What do you think of her eyes?'

'She has the most beautiful eyes.'

'Are they still beautiful?'

'Yes.'

'You're lying, Abraham. Time has made you blind. Do you really still love her?'

'Yes.'

'You're lying, Abraham. Love dies too. Either she's gone with another man or she's dead.'

Yusuf toyed with his beard and said:

'When men are on their own, they can be saints, but put them with women and they become the very devil. Some people count the passing of the days and others count the beats of their hearts; some grieve over their former days of beauty and others drive their cars looking backwards. The most beautiful things in this world finish up wrecked and crushed. This is a truth which I heard from a dumb man. O doctor of healing, why are you afflicted with leprosy...? O eye doctor, why is your eyesight so bad...?'

Between one wing and another, there lies flying!

They transferred me to another wing when a spare room became free—a private wing for civil servants and people with special privileges. Some of the patients used to come round from the wards to enjoy the peace and calm in our wing.

I discovered that some of my things were disappearing while I was out of my room. Everything that was eatable, smokable or drinkable started to vanish. Even the bottle of Martini disappeared out of my bag. I had a permit enabling me to leave the hospital grounds, so I was able to go into town to buy the things I needed. Nobody touched my books or magazines or newspapers. Once I came across a patient scoffing my private food and he shouted across to me from the hospital entrance:

'Come and have some. It's very good.'

I thanked him and left him to finish what must have been a pretty delicious meal: a farm chicken with onion and raisins. I let him eat his fill. He finished off with a banana and an orange, and afterwards he asked for a cigarette.

Damnati was the strongest patient in the hospital and he'd been there for over ten years. He'd previously worked in a German circus, where his act was an acrobatic routine that involved carrying six fully grown adults. He wasn't the longest-term resident in the hospital, though. Shama had been there for even longer: fifteen years. She'd got pregnant in the hospital three times, nobody knew by whom. When her sister visited her, she'd spit at her and insult her and then refuse to talk to her.

Mizmizi was brought back to hospital one morning with his head bandaged and his face all cut. He was one of the patients who was allowed to come and go as he pleased. He'd been in treatment for more than five years. He wasn't rough or aggressive with people. His problem was that he was stirred to craziness by the sight of broken objects. He was the one who took care of the hospital bitch, washing her and feeding her, and being friendly and playing with her. When he spent a few days in town, he'd sometimes get bored and head-butt one of the de luxe shop windows. And when he was particularly crazy, he'd chew bits of glass and razor blades, and in fact he did eventually die after swallowing a lump of glass. He quite often drank wine and smoked *kif* and swallowed tranquillizers, and in his actions he tended to project the state of his world onto others. He didn't live his tragedy on his own, unlike most of the other patients, who retreated into their own little worlds and suffered in isolation. It was extraordinary how cruel they could be to themselves! Mizmizi thought of the hospital as his real home. Nobody ever visited him. He had more friends in the hospital than he had on the outside. There was another patient who had no visitors either. He was a porter at the railway station, and he only came into hospital during the winter because that was the time when he was more or less unemployed.

With a view to putting an end to people pilfering my belongings, I asked Damnati to guard my room. He would sit in front of my door, idly thumbing through my magazines and newspapers, and smoking cigarettes which he rolled himself. I bought him a packet every two or three days, and I'd give him some of my food. Sometimes he'd take a book and pretend to be reading it, page by page, muttering aloud as he read, although in fact he couldn't read a single word. One day he asked me to read out loud to him. After a few paragraphs he stopped me:

'I used to read like that too, when I was in elementary school.'

When his poor mother visited him, which was every week or two, he'd act out celebrating his birthday with her. He'd sit on her knee as if he was her little boy, and shower her head and hands with kisses. He'd return to his seat for a moment or two and then begin the routine all over again. If any of the new patients happened to be passing and stared at them, they'd be rewarded with a punch in the face—a punch that was powerful but not usually enough to knock them unconscious. The older patients knew of his insane jealousy, so they gave him a wide berth. Damnati's punishment would be two or three days in solitary confinement in the high-security wing. Since I came to the hospital I'd saved him from it on two occasions—this involved paying the sum of 10 dirhams to the head nurse each time.

It was even possible to have sex with some of the female patients, paying in dirhams or whatever they happened to need. The hospital didn't need professional prostitutes coming in. During the night Damnati's madness took the form of guarding the toilets. The first time he did it, he stopped all the patients going in by lashing out and trying to hit them. Nothing could be done about it because the guard and the male night-duty nurse were nowhere to be found—they were presumably asleep or playing cards. In the morning, people were vomiting all over the place because they couldn't stand the smell of the patients who'd shat in their clothes and their beds. This time they put Damnati on electric shock treatment, to calm him down, as well as two days' solitary confinement. On the third day I freed him by the usual means, with a 10-dirham bribe. In fact outbursts of this kind were fairly rare with him.

I cut out pictures of naked girls from *Playboy* magazine and stuck them up round my room. The room had a small window looking down onto a grassy yard where the female patients walked during their recreation periods. They would chatter among themselves, or in scattered groups, or on their own. They would comb each other's hair and go through the motions of delousing each other, even if there wasn't a flea among them. When you watched the way they moved, they really did look like monkeys. When an argument broke out among them, they had a habit of baring their genitals. They'd grab each other's hair and pull it, and scratch and kick like furies. Whenever there was a fight, the others wouldn't step in to separate them, and if the warders didn't arrive in time the fighting would spread like wildfire. During the four months I spent in the hospital, I witnessed many scenes of violence between them, over the stupidest little things: someone asking someone else for a comb, or arguing over a place to sit, or because someone happened to look at someone else. 'Why are you staring at me like that?' One particular woman always went off on her own. She used to strip off her clothes and then start combing her hair distractedly. She came up to my window and asked for a cigarette. I gave her two or three, so as to stop her coming back. I didn't want to deprive her of her nakedness, or stop her smelling the bunch of flowers that she'd somehow managed to find.

At night another figure would materialize in the hospital. There were always one or two patients who couldn't get to sleep. The Virgin would often come to visit me during the hours of darkness, sometimes tearful and sometimes ecstatically happy. She came in wearing a flimsy nightdress. She was short and stocky, with her hair cut short. Her face was youthful and her complexion wheat-coloured. She had a neurosis because she was infertile. She was afraid she'd go mad.

'I know that I'm here, but this isn't the right place for me.'

She'd say this with a sigh. She drank and smoked eagerly, as a way of calming her tension. For her I could always spare some cigarettes and a drink or two. One night she stripped naked and struck a pose in imitation of one of the pin-up girls on my wall.

'Is she prettier than me?'

‘Not at all—but you’re not like her and she’s not like you.’

Sometimes she’d ask me to put on dance music for her, so I would, and she’d begin to dance, caressing her pretty body obsessively. She’d coyly take off some of her clothes and begin writhing on the bed like a snake. It was as if she was making love to her body, and she danced until the dancing tired her. Then she’d fling herself onto the bed, motionless. She sometimes stayed until it was almost morning, or she’d leave suddenly without saying goodbye. Her whole existence was wrapped up in the child she wasn’t able to have.

One morning Dr Monserrat summoned me to his office:

‘In my opinion the state of your health would have justified you staying for a week at most, but you’ve been here for four months now. I think you’ve had long enough. I’m not running a hotel, you know. It’s about time you got back to work.’

The Virgin began dancing and singing in a loud voice on my last night. The male duty nurse and the night warder came and took her back to her dormitory. The duty nurse had sex with her. When I went looking for her during the night, I found him on top of her in the laundry room. He said:

‘She’s all yours when I’ve finished.’

I slipped 10 dirhams into his hand and for a moment he slowed his humping.

21

Sarah

Sarah came from Larache to Tangier having slept with half the Spanish army in town, and after them the Moroccans. Her mother was Jewish and she'd married a Spaniard, but she hadn't renounced her religion, even though she wasn't a regular synagogue-goer. Her mother had seen her share of sexual goings-on in her youth. The Hotel Arcadia was the sum total of Sarah's wealth. She'd sold her bracelets, her rings and her gold chain to buy the deeds of the place, and she'd replaced her jewellery with paste imitations.

My neighbour at the time was a Danish actor by name of Henning. Both of us left our doors wide open. I was hoping to strike lucky with a woman and he was hoping for a man. Either one of us might have got our way because that's how it is with Tangier nights—full of passing surprises.

He sat reading classical drama, while I read whatever came to hand. He was going back over roles that he'd performed in Denmark more than ten years previously. I didn't understand a single word, but I found it quite moving to watch his performance and listen to the sound of his voice. One night he was kneeling down, playing a part, and when he stood up again he had tears in his eyes.

If we had no luck with our waiting, we'd keep each other company, either in my room or in his, and we'd share a jug of wine to pass the time. He was very emotional and highly strung.

On very hot days he was in the habit of standing stark naked in front of the mirror. On his 50th birthday he wasn't sure whether to laugh or cry. He drank himself more or less into a stupor, and as we carried him to bed he was mumbling like a kid:

'Leave me alone, you bastards!'

He was dependent on his aunt for his income. He had a monthly allowance from her, which gave him enough to be able to live in Tangier, or somewhere like it, for the rest of his days. Death terrified him. Once I found him crying in his room just because a funeral cortège had passed in front of his hotel. (In the late 1960s he suffered a brain haemorrhage in Melilla, and died and was buried there.)

I told him:

'If we want to conquer the idea of death, the important thing is not to imagine ourselves as dead. A person's destiny lies within himself. Don't depend on anyone and don't expect anyone to console you. Imagine that you're immortal. The only thing that defeats death is a love of life.'

This seemed to cheer him up a bit because he came right back at me:

'You must think I'm naive. What do you think this is, the theatre?'

Henning didn't seem to realize how sick he was. The slightest pain made him shudder.

Five or six of the permanent residents usually had lunch and supper in the hotel's small dining-room-cum-kitchen. Our cook, Lala Safiya, served the meals. When Sarah was in the mood, she'd serve us herself, and then she'd come and join us at our table. Lola, her mother (her real name was Hassiba), never joined us for anything. She just stayed in her gloomy room. Sometimes she played cards with herself. Hardly anyone ever visited her.

One day we were joined at our table by a character whom I'd seen at the café in the Inner Souq. I had no idea who he was. He had a kind of superior air about him, and I decided that he was just trying to give the impression of being someone important. He was a friend of one of Sarah's lovers—the black man Boutami, who was big-built with a face the size of half a melon, a narrow forehead and eyes like black grape-pips.

This newcomer wasn't staying in our hotel. As the days passed he seemed unable to break the ice with us. We would sit there joking and laughing, and he'd just scowl. I thought maybe he was wanting us to cheer him up. That night we finished supper and had a few drinks, and then we started telling jokes. By the end we were almost in tears from laughing so much, and then, all of a sudden, he got up and went stomping out. Hell, what happened to that kangaroo!

The next day he was the first person into the dining room. I found him thumbing through a French magazine, and in front of him lay an object wrapped in a sheet of newspaper. I said hello as I sat down and he responded with a curt nod. Then he bowed his head in silence again. I thought he looked like he was pretending to be Rodin's 'Thinker'. I almost burst out laughing. Lala Safiya was looking extremely worried, which wasn't like her at all. The door of the restaurant faced Lola's room. Sarah sometimes slept there with Lola when her boyfriend wasn't spending the night with her in the hotel. She came out and waved to me to come across. Something was obviously the matter. She ushered me into the room:

'What did you do to upset him? Don't you realize he's a big-shot policeman and a friend of Boutami's?'

'So what?'

'That thing wrapped in newspaper is a gun. Lala Safiya saw him bring it out and polish it.'

'So what's this got to do with me? Is he making trouble, giving you a hard time?'

'Of course not... but don't go doing anything to upset him. I hope you can just eat quietly together until you get used to him.'

'Or he gets used to us.'

'I hope I've made myself clear. I don't want problems, you understand?'

Sarah is the kind of person who shits herself when she has to deal with the authorities.

The elderly day porter, Don Juan, used to sit in a corner of the hallway. He was always teasing Sarah and cracking jokes about her. It amazed me how he got away with it, but then again he probably had nothing to lose. Once, when we were having supper together, he said, in his cheerful, mocking way:

'I see this chicken had no legs. Presumably it flew about all the time.'

On his plate was a wing and the neck of a chicken. He'd been working for Sarah for the best part of ten years.

On this particular day, around the table were Bouzian the English teacher, Henning, the police officer and myself. Don Juan didn't eat with us when he was in a bad mood—he'd wait until the restaurant was empty. Sarah looked in on us and then disappeared, looking worried and obviously waiting to see what would happen. Lala Safiya was more upset than her. She'd never seen a real gun in someone's hand before.

'He was polishing it like a pair of glasses!' she told me.

There was a brooding silence, which was unusual for us. Henning didn't know about the wrapped-up revolver. Sarah poured out the wine for us and then took the bottle back to the kitchen. Henning ordered another bottle, in an attempt to break the silence. He seemed worried that something was about to happen that night. He was probably miserable about his boyfriend too—they'd split up a few days previously. He seemed to take love more seriously when he was depressed than when he was in a good mood. He poured the policeman a drink with a shaking hand and then proceeded to pour drinks for us. We clinked glasses. Sarah and Lala Safiya seemed slightly less worried now and they watched us with strained smiles. I don't know why, but it struck me that Sarah looked like an ostrich. Was this on account of her long neck? Or maybe the fact that she had a heart-shaped face? The policeman ordered another bottle before the previous one was finished. He was trying to be friendly and he surreptitiously tucked his bundle away in the pocket of his coat.

Bouzian was pursuing a romance with a girl student of his. He'd never spoken to her; it was a case of love at a distance. Twice a week he started teaching at 10 in the morning, so on those days he had to leave for Tetuan at 6 o'clock and generally returned three hours later. He would go to the Café Avenue d'Espagne for breakfast, and when his newfound sweetheart passed the café, he got some sort of pleasure out of the fact that he could see her but she couldn't see him. When he returned tired and listless, we knew that he hadn't seen her pass that day. Anyway, on those particular days, whether she passed or not, he'd treat us to a bottle or two for supper. He only drank on social occasions. He wasn't up to drinking on his own: he drank to be sociable, as they say.

At around 1 in the afternoon a ladder appeared, together with a number of police and firemen, and a murmuring crowd outside. They had to break the window so as to get the door open from the inside. Sarah's face was pale and she was trembling. She was obviously very worried. Everyone who knew Justine was shocked that she'd committed suicide. She'd been perfectly happy when she'd left us. She'd had a good meal with us and she'd drunk until her cheeks were flushed. I remembered her last smile as she went up the stairs to her room. There were some days when the only food she had was bread soaked in wine. She spent most of her time reading. The cheque she received every month was late. It was getting her down, having to be so dependent on her parents' allowance. I'd invited her to join us for supper when I found out about her difficulties. I doubt that she committed suicide just because her cheque was late arriving. There must have been a lot of other problems—some much deeper unhappiness. But either way, she'd swallowed several tubes of tranquillizers. Perhaps the fact that she'd unexpectedly had such a good time with us was a contributing factor to her breakdown!

After the body had been removed and the police had left, Sarah burst into tears. I joined her in a glass of brandy in an attempt to cheer her up. We talked about fate, and people's destinies, and I forgot all about my school work. We laughed and got drunk together. I ended up in my room, fast asleep in all my clothes, and with no idea how I'd got there. I was woken up by a banging on the door, summoning me to supper. The restaurant had none of the cheerfulness that we managed to create on most nights.

During the school holidays Bouzian was thoroughly depressed. He was still going to Tetuan and coming back at the same time as usual. There was no sign of his girl student any more, but he was still looking out for her. I took him to Barghoutha's house. She had three girls and I let him choose. I went in with a girl who happened to know Tetuan, so I was able to talk about some of my haunts in the old days. In Dean's Bar afterwards I asked him about the girl he'd ended up with.

'She's a nice kid, but I didn't want sex with her because she told me the story of why she's a prostitute and it was rather sad.

Apparently she's got her mother to support and a 1-year-old baby daughter.'

I can't stand this kind of prostitute, who bring their worries into bed with them. They're a disaster...

Boutami was not Sarah's only lover, but he was the one who'd stayed with her over the years. Her sexual appetite brought in a variety of young studs from the city and elsewhere—some of them because they were poor and sexually frustrated, and some of them because they had a taste for foreign women, even if they were old like Sarah. On this particular day she had her favourite lover visiting, a young man from Shafshawan. He was in his 30s—younger than her son Carlos. It was Boutami's custom to spend Saturday evening and Sunday with her, through to Sunday evening. The rest of the week he spent with his wife and three daughters. But this particular day was a Monday. Maybe somebody'd told him there was a rival for her affections, so he'd come to sniff out the competition. Sarah was wearing her best clothes and was dripping with perfume. The young man joined us for supper. You wouldn't say he was short of an appetite—he was voracious. He didn't smoke and he didn't drink. Sarah liked to put on a spread when he was around, so our supper was a real banquet whenever he came. But she had ways of recouping this outlay! I'd heard tell that she'd been seen buying horse meat and donkey meat at the butcher's. This was probably true, because the meat she fed us was sometimes on the rubbery side, but it didn't worry me either way. The fact was, our board and lodging with her was among the cheapest in the Inner Souq.

Boutami went up with Sarah to one of the empty rooms. We heard the sound of shouting and insults. Shortly afterwards Boutami walked past the restaurant door, glaring at the young man furiously. Sarah went into her mother's room. When she came out, she was wearing dark glasses—to hide a black eye. As a woman she was stubborn, determined, good-looking and not the kind to be defeated. She carried on as if nothing had happened. She was absolutely the mistress of her own freedom and desires. They could quarrel as much as they liked, they could come and they could go, but she was mistress of her own patch. They could get angry and stamp out, but all of them came back in the end because she was a byword for generosity, for good times and good sex.

22

Visiting Friends

Midday, in the middle of summer. Bored. A sensible person would have gone to the sea, but I'm lazy about the sea. Hadn't been swimming for years. It wasn't the pleasures of drink that had kept me away from it: it was more the pleasures of serious reading, creative writing and writing letters to friends. Thinking about things and dreaming... I'd even given up taking a siesta because when I sleep in the afternoon I tend to wake up feeling sluggish in the stifling heat.

On this particular day I had a choice of things to do: I could visit Charles Le Chevalier, or Patricia, or Benito Jarra, who had returned from Mexico. Or I could go to one of the bars down by the beach, but the chattering and babbling of the drunks would just have made the heat worse. So I decided to visit Benito, whom I hadn't seen since his return.

He received me barefoot and was as welcoming as ever. He spent most of his time waiting around for the cheques which his rich mother sent him. We embraced warmly. He clapped me on the shoulder:

'The wine hasn't aged you yet. Seems to be doing you good, in fact.'

'You too—I see the coke hasn't finished you off yet.'

His *jubbah* was open at the front. This time he wasn't living in a big apartment: he had a single room in Benshouqi, overlooking the shore and part of the harbour, and Hadbat el Cherf, and the railway station. A few books and some sheets of paper lay scattered on the *taifor*. He took two cold beers from a bowl covered with a piece of sacking:

'This is my fridge.'

There was a strong smell of hash. He was looking pretty healthy. He always looked like this when he arrived back, but he usually came out in spots when he went back onto sniffing coke, smoking hash, eating *majoun* and drinking.

'And Valerie?'

'I caught up with her when I was in Las Vegas. She's married with two kids. She lives with her husband on the Ivory Coast. I reckon that's about as much as she was looking for. She's had enough of bust-ups and broken hearts.'

'Patricia's had a kid too, a daughter, with Giovanni. She hasn't gone back to living with him but they're still seeing each other.'

'I knew that. We had breakfast together at the Café Central this morning.'

I took a peek at the sheets of paper on the *taifor*.

'What are you writing?'

'A novel. This is my first go at prose. I'm having a hell of a job writing even a page a day. I probably need some crazy woman I can get carried away with. The only thing that helps my writing is when I'm arguing, either with myself or with someone else. I hardly write at all when I'm in a good mood. "A lively mind needs a troubled spirit," as Alfonsina Storni says.'

'What about Selma? Where's she now?'

'No idea. I don't know who dumped who. I didn't complete my holidays in Las Vegas, because while I was there I met a woman who was a dead ringer for her... same looks, same character. I sucked three poems out of her and fled before I ended up hating them and tearing them up.'

He picked up the papers from the *taifor* and passed them to me.

23

Le Chevalier

I was hating the summer. The heat was stifling and there wasn't a lot about it that was enjoyable. Even when I had the occasional good idea, the weather was so hot that it made me dizzy and the ideas evaporated like the morning dew. When I was a kid I used to enjoy the summer. I'm the kind who prefers the moist sand of the sea to the dry sand of the desert—I don't like wind and sand hitting you full in the face so that you can't see a thing. I'm not the sort to hang onto dreams, except when desires get the better of me, and I only tend to remember my anxieties when I sit down to write.

I found Le Chevalier sitting and looking depressed out in front of the Café Central. He called me over:

'I want to ask you a favour. I need you to give me a hand with something.'

This was the first time I'd ever heard him ask anyone round there for help. Evening was drawing on. He got up slowly and said:

'You know, when people like me get old, we find ourselves wishing we could start life all over again.'

As I sit here writing these notes I'm listening to the Ode to Joy from Beethoven's Ninth Symphony, and Chopin's First Nocturne. I'll leave it to the reader to imagine how they sound.

The heat in Le Chevalier's room was like an oven. There was a bottle of rosé on the table. He only ever drank water when he had no wine. He used to say jokingly that water was only for frogs and camels. He poured me a glass of the wine: it was warm and sour-tasting, and you could smell the cork in it. He pointed to a shabby suitcase near the bed.

'I didn't really want to trouble you... would you mind carrying this to the beach for me?'

'To the beach?' I said.

I wondered whether he was going ga-ga.

'I know it sounds strange, but just do what I ask. I won't tell you what's in it—you can see for yourself when we get there.'

As we walked, he asked me to slow down and wait for him. I'd never seen him as tired and pathetic as this. He was the sort of person who wouldn't complain even if there really was something wrong with him, but as we went along he stumbled and almost fell. His suitcase wasn't heavy. I found myself wondering what it could possibly contain. Several people were already on their way home, abandoning the beautiful Tangier evening; others were still enjoying the pleasures of its moist sands. We reached a spot on the beach and I opened the magical suitcase. It had various things in it. Some short stories, some of which he'd read to me previously. They'd never been published. A stack of faded photographs. Medals awarded in two world wars. He asked me to burn the lot without taking anything out of the case. The thought of this upset me. Needless to say, I would do what he asked, but I did ask if I could have one of the photos of him to keep. He was adamant:

'No. Please just do as I ask. Don't argue. We can take plenty of pictures of you and me together whenever you like.

As the blackened pages flew about, he gazed across at an evening horizon that was suffused with the colour of almond flowers. Here were memories going back more than sixty years, wiped out without pity or remorse. He seemed on the verge of tears. The redness of his face reflected the turmoil inside him. All of a sudden I began to see him in a new light. All the stories he'd read to me previously had been devoid of any literary imagination. They were simply unadorned accounts of things that had happened in his life. Everything in them was pre-cooked and ready-made. Obviously his isolation didn't help, as far as developing his literary talents was concerned. He was the kind of person who, when they read or hear something, always want to know whether it's true.

He had a particular aversion to going to church on Sundays and saints' days. By this time the only pleasure he had from life was from the past: for him, the good old days had ended in the late 1940s, despite the disasters of wars large and small. This was his unhappiness. After his retirement from the army he'd decided to take up auto-suggestive therapy. He'd been interested in it when he was younger. As far as I was concerned, it was all hocus-pocus, but I changed my mind when I saw him treat Sarah in my presence. He began by saying things and getting her to repeat them. Then he passed the palm of his hand over her belly, which seemed to take away her pain, to such an extent that she was able to get up from her sick bed.

Le Chevalier had been our doctor in pain and in sorrow, and now he was the one who was in pain. Once, when I was suffering from anaemia, he had prescribed meatballs of raw horse meat mixed with the yoke of a raw egg, garlic, spices and wine. I understood, through things he said to me, that it's not possible for people to live with memories that are of failure and betrayal. He had no memories that were worth living for. He'd become alienated from everyone close to him, and they'd effectively killed him off while he was still alive.

His allowance cheque was more than usually late in arriving. He was getting depressed. He wouldn't look you in the eye. This was unusual for him. I heard him mumble:

'In the land of promises the poor man died of hunger.'

I didn't ask what he meant. As I left I wondered what it would be like to be 75. If it was ordained for me to live that long, I wondered what pleasures or miseries life would have in store for me. That earlier phrase of his kept coming back to me, obsessively: 'When we get old, we find ourselves wishing we could start life all over again.' So as to dispel the gathering gloom I told myself that I would never get old like that. I never met anyone of his age who didn't complain about time robbing him of the things he loved doing, or complaining about life itself. But Le Chevalier wasn't the kind of person to complain about his lot. I began to dread the end of my life as I saw it foreshadowed in his life. There's nothing worse than comparing your life with other people's lives.

As it turned out, there was a three-week delay in his allowance cheque arriving. The silent drop is the drop which breaks the silence. He had to cut back on food until he was eating only butter, tomatoes, onions and lemons. On most days I got a bottle of wine to share with him, out of sympathy for the poor man having to drink the water that he found so repellent. The French Cultural Centre invited him to give a lecture on auto-suggestive therapy, but his enthusiasm evaporated when he saw only about ten people in the hall, so he shortened his presentation to twenty minutes. This earned him 500 dirhams, which was enough to ward off poverty while he waited for his cheque to arrive. That evening he treated me in the restaurant of the hotel where we lived: food and drink, conversation and jokes, to while away the tedium of the night.

Last year he was disappointed in one of his ambitions. He was at the Café Zagourah, and he had asked the lady pianist and her violinist husband to accompany him in an old song from the 1930s. As soon as his voice began to ring out, all the passers-by began stopping outside the café. The waiter politely asked him to stop because singing was not allowed. I suppose reality had deserted Le Chevalier because he lived in a world that was foreign to him. He was like a man hanging from a branch over an abyss, weighed down by his burden of sadness.

He found me at the Café Central enjoying a morning of idleness. His depression had left him. He invited to go with him to visit his friend Georges, in Dahiyat 'Awama. It was a scorching day and I had nothing better to do with my time, so I went along. He bought a rabbit and some wine, a tin of mushrooms and some barley bread. We took the bus. From the last stop we still had about a kilometre to walk to reach Georges' little smallholding. The road was scorching hot under our feet. A small snake, about half a metre long, was crossing in front of us. Le Chevalier stopped and struck up a conversation with it:

He said: 'Go ahead, you cross first... You were here before us,' and he told me not to move.

The sweat was dripping from us. Georges earned his living from keeping bees. Hardly anyone ever visited him except for Le Chevalier, and myself when I went with him. Sometimes I bought honey from him. He was clearly delighted as he welcomed us. It was a tin hut, fairly roomy, that he'd built himself. It was stiflingly hot in summer and freezing cold in winter. His entire wealth consisted of livestock in the shape of cows and chickens. He led an abstemious life. The only furniture he owned was a bed, a table, some chairs and a small radio.

I felt like strolling in the shade of his orange and pear trees. Some of the pears were over-ripe and several had been eaten into by insects. I ate two that had fallen from the tree. Georges and Le Chevalier cooked the rabbit. I thought it best to leave them alone. Given that they were both of French origin, they had a lot in common. Le Chevalier was an unbeliever and Georges a believer, but they had an understanding. I never once heard them argue about religion. Georges had planted two wooden crosses, one in the field and the other near the well, and over the door of the hut he had another cross, made of dark wood, which looked more like a scarecrow. There was no room for Satan there! I wondered how he could possibly be happy in this almost total isolation. He had no books except for a few faded grey volumes. No sign of any newspapers or magazines. He probably nourished himself with meditation, like saints and hermits. Small birds were flitting between the trees. A black bird sat on a branch. It began to quiver and sing. It was probably a starling. I thought of Aïn Khabbès, and Busatin Kaytan, and the Sirimin fields in Oran. A person is how he ends his life, not how he begins it. That was another of Le Chevalier's sayings. If I lived that long, I wondered what kind of old age would await me. For sure I wouldn't end up burning a caseful of my memories on the beach.

Up until that point, I'd never allowed any emotion to betray me. I'd always lived in a kind of state of emergency. I only loved what was fleeting. Love, in fact, didn't interest me unless it was big and fantastic, like in a book. I spoke about it without touching it or embracing it. And most of the young women who attracted me were hermaphrodites. Deep down I probably had a hidden tendency to homosexuality. For me a woman's greatest attraction was probably her youth. I also found that the negativity of some women inspired nothing but an impulse of rape.

I'd been looking for life's games and symbols, not its reality; looking for the obscure and the riddle, not the clear and the simple; the unknown and not the known, the mirage and not the water. A very ripe pear fell to the ground next to me. It rolled towards me, so I picked it up. I ate it, thinking of Isaac Newton, and Henry Thoreau, and Robert Frost. I also thought of the Jew who threw himself out of a sixth-floor window in Tetuan. He landed on top of a Moroccan labourer and drove his head and neck into his chest. I prefer the cow mooing to the sound of a nightingale singing. The shadow of that tree carried me back to the shadowy greenery of my childhood: Aïn el Qetiout, Aïn el Hayani, Aïn Khabbès—all springs where I had drunk the water of cold and muddy misery.

This was the first time, as an adult, that I'd lain down to relax and think in a tree-filled, sunny spot like this. Previously I'd always walked straight past trees and only ever stopped to pick their fruit. Now I was enjoying a tree's shelter and feeding on its maturity. Time was no longer my prison. I was beginning to be able to hold it at bay whenever I wanted. I was grateful to my friend Le Chevalier. If it hadn't been for him, I wouldn't have experienced this intoxicating surge of memories which flooded me with their gentleness, their softness and their depth. My tiredness melted from me in a sensation of total, delightful relaxation, which then gave way to a delicious sleep.

Georges brought me an earthenware tumbler filled with wine. He was a real old-timer in everything he did, this amiable Georges—so gentle in his voice and his movements. As I sat and smoked, I began to see things more clearly with every sip of the wine. The various stages of my life seemed to parade before my eyes: the old and the new, the bad and the good, the pleasant and the painful—an intricate interweaving of light and shade, like the branches of this pear tree. A breeze began to blow, bringing a pleasant coolness with it. Le Chevalier called me over to eat. He always enjoyed his cooking. Rabbit cooked with wine and mushrooms was his special favourite. He really was rooted in this nomad-like life of his.

24

Patricia

To be honest, I don't much care for my next-door neighbour. She's the superficial kind who'd jump into bed with you as soon as look at you. At the moment I'm writing these diary notes in one of the new bars in Tangier, and what an ugly place it is! There are plenty of these new-style bars in the city now. Does this mean that the time has come for us to say goodbye to the Tangier nights of old? No—never! Tangier nights are part of my being. Once you've lived this city, you can only leave her if the umbilical cord is cut. How many times have I returned to her regardless of all the changes she's spawned? And how many times have I walked out on her, only to return before I'd got halfway down the road? The only truth lies in what the future holds for us. These days nobody takes responsibility for what they say. I like my solitude in the night, though. There nobody can reach me or bother me.

'Porco Giuda! Porco Giuda!'

Little Anastasia was crying. Why was she crying? Why was Patricia swearing and cursing like that—and more to the point, who was she swearing at? The heat was stifling. Anastasia was naked to the waist. I always find the nakedness of children particularly attractive. She put me in mind of a bouquet of red roses guarded by white flowers—white flowers with just a trace of red in them. I thought what a mixture there is of delight and unhappiness in our childhood. And after that, all we're left with is our dreams. After childhood what more can we do except practise the madness of the night?

Patricia was sitting on a mat, wearing a flowing *jubbah* she'd bought in Marrakech. She was breaking up a Virginia cigarette to make her joint—one of her 'rockets', as she called them. Was this some kind of suicide trait, or a statement about herself, or was it just for the pleasure of the thing? Maybe it was a protest. Maybe it was frustration. Then again, maybe it was nothing at all—just a way of passing the time. I think of the long nights I used to spend with her, with Keith Jarret playing in the background. When the rains come, there's always a chance you'll be flooded out, but in the end you don't usually drown.

Patricia was born to make others happy. On occasion I would inquire about the men in her life. She looked at me and smiled, but didn't answer. She just carried on rolling her joint, with her eyes lowered. The beauty of all women seemed to have come together in her. She had such a fine, tranquil presence that it would have made a woman-lover of any woman-hater, and a stallion of the impotent. After a while she said innocently:

'Of course there are others, but what does that matter?'

When I was with her I found that I developed more of a love for myself. Dance, dance and make the world a beautiful place! Despite the fact that Patricia was a pretty terrible poetess, she inspired the most beautiful poetry in those who came to know her.

Patricia's face was all smiles. Anastasia stopped crying and came over to me. She was glad to see me. Patricia said:

'You've arrived at just the right moment. Anastasia was wanting someone to give her a cuddle.'

I took her up in my arms. What is life? Life is taking risks. Like flying in planes. Ever since I'd first heard the roar of an aircraft, I'd always dreamed of flying in one.

Most of the dreams that I remember were always to do with flying. I'd be flying over a forest and come in to land in front of a cave, and I always dreamed that I was the only person who knew about this cave. It gave me pleasure to think that I was there all on my own, far from the smells of humanity, because I'd become sick of the world and the world had become sick of me...

Anastasia snuggled up to me. Her mother loved children, but

she didn't have much patience in the business of bringing them up.

'Were you swearing at Anastasia?' I asked.

'Goodness, no! How could you even think such a thing? I wasn't swearing at anyone at all. It's just my way of letting off steam. I was probably swearing at myself without realizing it. I don't know...'

I had my first swim. The sea had been storing up the summer's heat all through the season. There are people in this world who do idiotic things from the moment they wake up and there are others who are born lazy, live lazy and die lazy, to the intense irritation of everyone else.

Sitges! It would be good to see her dusk again and her white alleys in the night! There I saw lovers bickering over letters that hadn't arrived and had probably never been sent. What is left to us except a twilight that reminds us of tendernesses near and far?

Patricia took a draw on her joint and asked me:

'What's going on out in the street?'

'The same as every year. Ready-made slogans, all censored in advance before they're shouted. This year they're protesting about the amount of new building going on in the city. But who's responsible for all the building in the first place? They allow Labour Day to go off peacefully every year, but it's all hypocrisy. This is just a masquerade of democracy!'

'They're right, though, Choukri. Tangier has literally begun giving up her ground in a search for some imaginary heaven. We're all suffering from the way the city's being invaded and spoiled. So we're trying to start things afresh so as to discover our identity. But when you go hunting a butterfly in the forest, you might just get bitten by a poisonous snake, and the man who goes out fishing might just get eaten by a shark.'

Patricia was a strange mixture of happiness and sadness, of contentment and complaints. I wouldn't argue with her. I stepped outside the smoky room so as to get Anastasia out of the hash-filled air. She held onto my shoulder tightly. It was obviously true that she needed somebody to cuddle her. Le Chevalier once told me:

'Whenever I'm away from my friends, I find that I feel closer to them and they become closer to me. When people are together all the time, they can't be bothered with each other. Most people see barriers even when there are no barriers there.'

I pointed to the hut that had belonged to Tomás El Rojo.

'There used to be an old Spaniard living there. He died several months ago. I used to know him.'

'I hope he was happy in the way he lived.'

Anastasia had fallen asleep by now. I laid her on the little bed. Patricia passed me the joint. She gave the impression of being all misty and romantic, but she knew how to enjoy life's pleasures.

'So what was the old man's story?'

'He hated Franco and he used to go round the streets selling balloons to the children.' (I was talking to her outside the room.)

'Is that all there was to him?'

'What more do you want?'

'He was living a life of silence and exile.'

'Should he have been doing more?'

'You always talk about old people like they're the most wonderful thing in the world. But it seems the times of the prophets are past!'

'How was Benito when you saw him this time?'

'We had breakfast together at the Café Central.'

'I know. He told me.'

'He read me his three latest poems. He seems to have lost his poetic spontaneity. Now he's starting to intellectualize things. He's still dabbling in epicureanism.'

'I thought he was going to become a Sufi. Why can't he make his mind up?'

'Good question! Anyway, tell me about your friend Le Chevalier.'

'He's still in the land of the living. He's pretty depressed these days, though. He's got a brother in Australia and they write to each other once in a while.'

Le Chevalier thinks his brother behaved disgustingly by leaving his wife and going off to Australia with another woman. But then his brother wrote to him from Australia and told him that out there everyone cheats on their partners. It was nothing unusual for husbands and wives to take up with lovers from the days when they were young. Charles Le Chevalier's wife had died, and their children had married and had children of their own. His brother's wife was living out her declining years in Louvain, all on her own.

Patricia went off with some other hippies at the start of the 1970s and never came back to Tangier. Last summer a young Italian came to visit me. He told me that he knew Patricia and that she'd been diagnosed with a malignant brain tumour. Her daughter was studying at university. I wrote her a letter, by way of saying goodbye, but that was the last I heard of her.

25

A Mental Block

Qasem was his mother's only son. He lived with her, but although he supported her, at the same time he was entirely dependent on her. He obeyed her as a mother, but he was unable to convince himself that she had repented of certain of her past ways. He loved her and he hated other women. When he was with her he had moments of calm, and in those periods he could enjoy the memories of his past. His childhood was a place of brightness and light, like a secret lake, but somewhere there lurked some terrible mental block. He was befuddled with weird misconceptions, unable to break free from them. Fear paralysed his senses and his brain somehow seemed to work on a logic of its own. He had this tendency of shrouding everything that happened to him in gloom. He didn't have the strength to derive courage from his fear. He was a prisoner of his mental block. Any affection lessened his misery, but his friends were few and far between.

One night we got him drunk in the house of one of those friends. A girl volunteered her services more or less as a prostitute, in an attempt to snap him out of this blockage. There wasn't much chance that she'd succeed, but it was worth a try. As it turned out, he would have throttled her if we hadn't managed to break into their room. On another night he started hitting his mother, with anything he could lay his hands on. This was the first time, but by no means the last, because it tended to recur every time he got drunk and fell out with a woman. He was used to getting affection from his mother, but wasn't capable of finding it in other women. He didn't want to spend the whole of his life as an object of pity, but on the other hand he wasn't able to break out of his mental block. He was always worried about people thinking badly of him. He felt nauseous when he thought of anything even slightly risky that might lead him into the unknown, and this just reinforced his mental block. It was very rare for him to come to the café, and when he did he always insisted on sitting by the door: this was another of his phobias. He used to walk a lot, to help work off his nervous tension. His route would be across the beach or to Jebel el Kebir.

He used to visit me once or twice a week. We weren't close friends but I felt sorry for him and we would compare notes on our jobs. He taught French and I taught Arabic. His interest in French literature began with Madame de Stael and ended with Mallarmé. We listened to classical music together. His favourites were the Pathétique, Scheherazade, Don Giovanni and the Eroica. His presence was never disturbing if you were someone who preferred silence. I used to read or write and he'd sit and listen to the music. Sometimes he'd sigh and look at me, but I pretended not to notice. Sometimes he'd stare at me absent-mindedly too. I went out of my way to avoid making him feel uncomfortable. He'd recover his peace of mind while I carried on reading or writing, and sometimes I closed my eyes and pretend to be similarly deep in thought.

His mother's past was a constant source of shame to him. She'd sold her young body so as to provide him with a future, but he couldn't bring himself to forgive her past. In the end she'd given up men and taken a job as a cleaner in a hotel. This was at about the time he became a teacher. By that time she was about 50, and he was getting on for 30. He always carried a photograph of her as a young woman. He had a bee in his bonnet, that anyone who was about the same age as her, man or woman, must know about the profession she'd practised in her youth. A woman in the street had once asked casually about his mother and he'd got angry:

'Why do you ask? Where do you know her from? Is she a relation of yours?'

So it came to the point that nobody dared ask him anything about her.

He took out a picture of his mother and passed it to me:

'Do you know her?'

I looked at her and then at him:

'No.'

'You've never seen her?'

'Never.'

I returned it to him and inquired innocently:

'Who is she?'

He said, in some confusion:

'I don't know. I found it in one of my books. I don't know who put it there.'

He'd tried in vain to remove his mother from Tangier so that they could live in one of the northern towns—Asila, Larache, Qasr el Kebir, Tetuan, Shawan... anywhere she fancied. But his mother insisted on living and dying where she was born.

Anyway, on one particular evening he came to visit me. I could see that he wasn't his usual self. He wasn't even enjoying his favourite music. I began to feel uneasy. I was beginning to wish I'd never met the man. I had a feeling that something out of the ordinary was about to happen. I was sitting reading a novel—*Perfume*, by Patrick Suskind, in a Spanish translation. All of a sudden, as if it was the most normal thing in the world, Qasim took out a ratchet knife, and the clicking sound as he opened it notch by notch was matched by the pounding of my heart. Why was he picking on me? Was he trying to frighten me just for the sake of it? Or was he planning some mad crime born of despair? But why me of all people? There was no quarrel between us. The only thing I knew about his mother was what I'd heard about her. I was the same age as her. That was all. There was absolutely no reason for him to have taken against me.

A record of the Pathétique was on the turntable as he casually tapped his nails with the blade of the knife. I got up without looking at him, and went to the kitchen to fetch the cutting board that I use for cutting meat, and a knife. Then I opened the fridge and took out a leg of lamb. I put the board on the table and began cutting up the meat with the same calm, nervy movement, as if playing a game, while he picked at his nails with his knife. Each of us was looking at the other with an air of defiance: a mixture of mockery and fear. I'd never experienced such a crazy scene in all my life. I was on the verge of becoming as crazy as him. I think I really was wanting the scene to turn violent. I wanted to test myself. A showdown: either him or me. I stopped smoking my cigarette and put it in the ashtray. Then I returned to cutting up the meat. It crossed my mind that I should have jumped on him, smashed the chopping board across his head and carved him up just like the leg of lamb. That would have stopped his nonsense. He was following my movements absent-mindedly. Then, in the same calm, playful, slightly theatrical way in which he'd taken out the knife in the first place, he closed it and returned it to his pocket. I plunged my fingers into the meat and then licked them greedily. He left me, silently, without saying goodbye. As he was halfway out he looked at me and smiled nervously; then he laughed out loud and went out. I laughed too.

That night his mother was screaming and yelling for help even more than usual. When we saw her, her clothes were torn and her face was scratched. She was crying, but she wouldn't say anything to explain what had happened. As another neighbour was leaving her, she heard her say:

'He came out from my belly, that much I know, but he's not human, he's a devil.'

About two years later I was returning from Rabat to Tangier and the bus stopped at Larache bus station. I got out to get a drink. There was Qasem, barefoot and bearded. He was disgustingly dirty. He was picking up dogends here and there, and had a lighted one in his mouth. In his left hand he was carrying a tattered book. I left my drink and went into the café to buy some cigarettes for him. I wasn't gone for long, but by the time I got back he'd vanished. I looked for him all over the bus station. Not finding him, I asked the waiter where he might be.

'He sleeps in the old Christian graveyard. They call him the "philosopher".'

The bus driver was sounding his horn, signalling that he was ready to leave. I climbed on board.

26

The Majorca Hospital

I hadn't realized that Latifu was gay until that particular evening. It was a weird evening, but I don't think he'd set it up deliberately. He had a young teenage boy with him. We were drinking in the Café Roxy, which was where I'd got to know him some months previously. I had no sense of the days and weeks passing during that period because I was drinking really heavily. My only memories were of confusion and delirium. Latifu suggested that we go back to my place for a drink, and I nodded in agreement. I was just about ready to pass out but I went along with it. Looking back, I think I must have had a gut feeling that something was about to happen that night.

He went out and came back carrying a bottle of wine and a few beers. We went to my flat and began partying, mixing the wine with the beer. Latifu kissed his boyfriend and started messing about with him. The boyfriend let himself go, without paying any particular attention to me. Then he gave me a look that suggested he was prepared to be shared. Latifu whispered that he was game too. I indicated that I wasn't interested. I went to the kitchen, picked up a knife and put it in my pocket. Latifu opened the door. He had my radio-cassette player in his hand. I remember that John Lennon was singing 'Imagine' on the radio. I leapt across and grabbed Latifu by the arm.

'You'll leave the cassette player where it belongs.'

The teenager wandered off, like a cat sensing danger. I locked the door. Latifu pushed me and I banged against the fridge. I pulled the knife out of my pocket. He dropped the casette player and rushed out onto the balcony. This gave him plenty of space to dodge around among the washing. Although I didn't realize it at the time, I tried to stab him in the belly. Because he tried to protect himself, he took the full force of the blow on his hand. I started lashing out in a blind frenzy. It was as if it wasn't me who was doing it—it was the wild animal lurking in every human being who has ever stabbed someone. He began yelling. I thought of the neighbours and I stopped. I stood back to give him space so that he could get out. I lashed out and kicked at him as he passed, and then I locked the door. I paced about between the two rooms and the balcony in a state of theatrical frenzy, slashing at the air with the knife as the wild, starving, craving animal in me slowly subsided. I threw the knife from the balcony down into the street. I was in such a state of depression that I could have ended up stabbing myself too. I went to sleep with all my clothes on, at one point breaking into a fit of hysterical crying. I dreamed of heads being cut off, and blood spurting out of their veins and then drying up, and of bellies ripped open and eyes gouged out.

In the morning I was woken by a knock at the door. There were bloodstains on the walls. I was shaking all over as I went to answer. It turned out to be Abdelmalek, the owner of the building. He didn't ask me what had happened. I put myself into his hands. I mumbled:

'Take me to Tetuan. The Majorca Hospital. Dr Ja'idi. I know him. I'll be safe with him.'

I woke up at about 2 in the morning in a room with a number of patients in it. At last—a chance to get away from it all. Far away from all the people I'd ever known. To hell with lousy humanity! I smoked a couple of cigarettes. The man sleeping on my left woke up. I gave him a cigarette too, which he smoked with evident pleasure. We talked about sleep, and how many hours people need, and we agreed on the fact that sleep in hospital (and in prison) is not the same as sleep in your own home. The hospital was completely quiet. Suddenly a woman appeared and started pacing up and down the corridor. She stared at us sullenly. She was probably suffering from insomnia and hadn't taken her sleeping pills. I was in a relaxed frame of mind. Another woman woke up and switched on a radio. My neighbour, a man from Amran told me:

'They robbed her son in Fez and then they killed him. He was 12 years old.'

In the morning a flock of patients, both male and female, arrived at our room. They took turns at coming in. They'd obviously heard there was a new patient. Abdelmalek had given me a handful of loose change. A good-looking woman patient was giving me the come-on. She asked me for that most coveted of objects in a hospital—a cigarette. Suicide hadn't helped her. She'd swallowed a whole load of sleeping pills and then swallowed the bottle too. She reminded me of Mizmizi in the Beni Makadah Hospital. I wrote these notes at various different times—these ones at 5 in the morning. I had a permit allowing me to leave the hospital. I only left in order to buy basic provisions, because people's faces on the outside struck me as stupid and unpleasant. In the hospital people's faces were actually made more beautiful by the misfortunes and worries that they'd endured in their lives. Hospital bread has its own particular taste. These mental patients opened the doors of inspiration for me, enabling me to look out onto the world. Whenever I looked at one of the crazy people there, I saw a hidden flame of intelligence as old as humanity itself. There you saw the full extent of human distress. I heard the screams of a young boy crying:

'No, no, take me to Martil! Martil, Martil!'

Abdelhakim spoke to me for the first time. He told me:

'Whoever comes to us is our brother. And those who do *not* come, they are our *true* brothers.'

He gave me a cigarette. My soul had been absorbed by the soul of el Mahdi ibn Tawmart.

'You're a lucky man,' I said.

'I have something to ask you.'

'What is that, O wise one?' (This was how I'd begun to address him.)

'I want a white *djellaba*, so that I can pass judgement fairly. This ring which you see here was loaned to me by Solomon the Wise, and he commanded me to judge with it.'

'But judges nowadays do their judging in black robes.'

'They have not yet received the vocation of whiteness.'

Najib said:

'I long for that which is eaten more than I desire to eat it. I don't want to be a rose or a dried twig to be burned. I want to become a grain of sand. Grains of sand are more similar to each other than flowers and twigs.'

One of the patients came into our room and said:

'The rain falls upon us like a stone.'

Another patient dropped a carton of milk and it burst. He kicked the carton and wandered off. Another one stood up, went towards him and started throwing dirt at him.

Miloud said:

'I left my village barefoot, and arrived in a strange country barefoot, so how had I benefited from the journey? I met barefoot people and foreigners like myself. Our road was different but our exile was one and the same. They don't use firewood for heating. And they always bolt even their windows. And every door has an eye in the middle of it, like the eye of a dead fish. Who can bring himself to knock on their doors? Oh what a thing it is to be a foreigner in the cities! Then we long to be in huts in the mountains and the open deserts. There the stranger can always count on finding shelter.'

Every day I regularly lent Soraya a dirham for the day. She had a habit of waking up every morning at 3 o'clock on the dot. She also had an obsession with cleaning the corridor and the rooms in our wing. Nobody could stop her. She'd wake me up every night to give me back the dirham she'd borrowed from me during the day. One night I was annoyed at being woken up, but when I said as much she began crying and protested:

'I'm like a sister to you but you don't love me!'

I tried in vain to persuade her that I didn't want her waking me up when she came round on her cleaning jaunts. She was sitting on the ground smoking a cigarette thoughtfully. I regretted my outburst, but she still carried on borrowing a dirham from me during the day and returning it at 3 in the morning. I'm convinced it was always the selfsame dirham that she'd borrowed in the first place. Nobody told Soraya to do her nightly cleaning rounds. It was just her particular obsession. She would talk to herself, mumbling incoherently. One night I asked her:

'Who's still awake in the other rooms?'

'Everyone's asleep. Only the ghosts aren't sleeping.'

Bahi's brother gave me three or four packs of cigarettes and asked me to look after them for his brother. If he'd put them straight into his hands, the other patients would have smoked the lot in a day. I gave him four or five cigarettes twice a day and he'd smoke them one after another without a break. Every time he saw me he promised that he'd leave me in his will a she-mule and some old money from the 1930s that he'd buried under a cactus bush somewhere. He seemed to live in the 1930s. His favourite food was fried egg. When his brother brought him in eggs, he didn't usually eat the hospital food. Generally he'd eat this meal with Wadrasi, and seeing that both of them had been in the hospital for a long time, they'd fall into conversation about matters of mutual interest.

They were both bedouins. Whenever they got together, their conversation tended to get heated. Once I was sitting close to them while they were eating. Suddenly Wadrasi poked Bahi in the left eye. This resulted in quite a scratch, and the blood started flowing from under the eye, but the conversation carried on regardless. I called over one of the male nurses. He patched it up and they both continued with their food and their conversation as if nothing had happened. There was no bad feeling between them. And the male nurse didn't say a word either. When they finished their food, Wadrasi gave Bahi a kiss on the head, thanked him and left. I gave Bahi three cigarettes and left him to enjoy them. He lit them one after the other until they were all finished.

Abdelmalek brought me a white *djellaba* from Tangier. I gave it to Abdelhakim, and I bought him a bar of soap to wash with. He began parading around our wing in his new garment. Then he went to the second wing, but when he tried to get into the third wing—the wing containing the 'shitters in their clothes', as they called them—Bu'nani, the hospital security guard, blocked his way. Abdelhakim had learned a bit of karate and he tried to fight back, but Bu'nani was strong, with a bear-like body. By the time they'd finished fighting, Abdelhakim's *djellaba* was torn and splashed with blood. I asked him:

'How could you let him tear your *djellaba*?'

'Don't worry about me—his face is more torn than my *djellaba*.

You should see the blood on his face.'

'So what are you going to do about the *djellaba*? You can't start passing judgement until you patch it up. Your sentence wouldn't be just.'

'Give me the price of a needle and thread. I shall just have to defer the matter that's awaiting judgement and postpone the visit that I'm expecting.'

'Whose visit is that?'

'He who was to prepare me for the judgement.'

Soraya had been round earlier, asking me for the usual dirham. Since it was evening, she'd be asleep now, all ready to wake me, as usual, when she got up to do her cleaning and return the dirham to me. It was drizzling, there were clouds in the sky and one of the patients was singing:

'The night is our night—where are you, O night?'

I spent two days with my family. There was still an icy silence between me and my father. Just to keep my mother happy, I kissed his head as usual, without a word passing between us. The pain that I'd had from him in my childhood, he was now getting back from me in his old age. There was no way that there could ever be a compromise between us. I wanted to take a look at the streets of my childhood. I thought of Bu'asa, in his drunken frenzy, with his eyes rolling up in his head, and Ezra Kun, and the maniacal Mr Mufaddal, and other characters who'd vanished into oblivion along with their names. My only childhood friends still remaining in town were Comero and Batati. At the entrance to Bab el Nawadir I was surprised to see Abdelhakim. He was walking along with a stick in his hand and a gang of children following in his wake. So he had escaped! He stopped his little gang. I asked him:

'Where to, O wise one?'

'To the hospital, if Allah wills.'

'And those children?'

'They are my helpers.'

'What are you intending to do?'

'We shall set free our brothers there.'

'And where are your weapons?'

'Stones. We shall fight the new with the old. Why don't you come along with us.'

'I'm going back to Tangier. I'm intending to do the same as you, to liberate our brothers there.'

'Convey my greetings to them.'

I slipped 20 dirhams into his hand. He embraced me and wished me luck. Then he went on his way again, with his acolytes following on behind.

27

A Mother's Death

Between the blind man and the person who sees, there's a difference in the perception of things. At least, that's the opinion of those who can see. What can a son say about the death of his mother? Everything and nothing. Do we know the sea from a drop of water? Or the desert from a grain of sand? Is a wild rose the whole of the forest? Is this like the man who dreams of travelling but never travels? Or one who sows without waiting for the sowing season? For my part, I have no ambition to own lots of money or to father generations of descendants. Words have become confused and the giants of literary inspiration are all dead. We have only our own intelligence to save us from inertia and stagnation.

There was a non-stop ringing on my doorbell, accompanied by the sound of someone banging on the door. Whoever it was, they were very determined. Was it just one of those things that happen in the night or was somebody deliberately trying to annoy me? Who knows! Mostly you don't make your enemies—either they make themselves or other people create them for you. And the real bore is that there are always plenty of volunteers for the job. At that unearthly hour of the morning I decided it must be a prostitute or something. This wasn't the first time I'd had people banging on my door, but the previous time it hadn't been so loud and insistent. Then it had been a woman off the streets, looking for a cigarette.

She was a hashish smoker, bent on oblivion and caring nothing for the realities of past or future.

The ringing and the banging became one continuous noise. It didn't have this urgency last time. I was still drunk. It was June. Summer no longer meant anything for me. A nothingness. The pleasures of summer had all been in the past, when I was young. Probably what had gone wrong was just in my head. During the summer I eat less and sleep less. What I once called a lie I hold as truth today. When are lies true? And the dissipation which is what gives cities their character? True beauty is created by catastrophe! I have heard this said by experts in urbanism. The woman model who strips naked to be painted doesn't arouse the artist's desire. One's living of life and one's understanding of it do not correspond in time. Probably life's most beautiful aspect is its delusions.

The sea washes at my feet. I wet my body with sea water and look to the horizon—at the sky, and at the sand, then at the blue waters stretching into the distance and enticing me into adventures that might prove fatal. On three previous occasions I have taken risks with the sea, and each time I came close to drowning. Once Benboukar and his friend Floris[1] rescued me on the Martil beach. Today I limit myself to splashing my head with a handful or two of water. I am no longer lured by the attractions of turquoise and lapis lazuli. Not at all.

Whoever it was, they were now ringing and knocking at the same time. Another stupid woman. Wait, can't you?! It's strange, the way I was always taking refuge in one last drink, and a bed for another fuck. A diver once told me:

'Rely on your imagination when you're waiting for someone and they don't turn up. If they don't turn up, just forget about them. It's more important to be close to yourself than to hang about waiting for others.'

Now the knocking had turned into a wild banging.

I often get people coming to Tangier who have no sea in their own towns. All our city means for them are the tourist streets, the cafés and the sex bars, the music and the brothels. That's all Tangier represents for them. All they're interested in is cunt and

---

1. Two boxers who lived in Tetuan in the 1940s.

arse. All they want is to get laid. My big weakness is getting drunk with my guests. I was regularly drinking myself to the point of stupidity, babbling away—and all the time my mother was dying in my absence.

No electricity because they've been trying to save on electricity bills. Ringing and knocking at the same time. Some crazy woman. Probably thrown out of a nightclub somewhere, completely penniless. An actor once told me:

'You seem to attract the friendship of women more than the friendship of men.'

In fact I'm only friends with myself.

'Open the door. It's 'Aqil!'

So that's who it was... My brother-in-law! Whatever'd happened, it must have been pretty serious for him to turn up at that time of night.

'Your mother's dead.'

In a voice that was hoarse with drunkenness I said:

'She's dead?'

'Yes. Get dressed quickly.'

I poured water over my head in an attempt to shock my system back into shape. This was the trouble with guests who drink more than you do. You end up in a pitiful state. They return to their cities after their holidays and I'm left here, wrecked. They did the same thing with Scott Fitzgerald and Jack Kerouac, drawing them into the heavy drinking which subsequently killed them. My relationship with these people means that I have to carry on with them, but I must find a way to break the cycle. Henry Thoreau built a hut in the Walden forest and began writing about ants and the smells of the forest, despising the stale air of offices. He really did prefer the smell of dung in fields to the perfumes of the grandest hotels.

It was 5 in the morning. 'Aqil's car was solid and new. He drove at speed, but he wasn't a reckless driver. I'm not in the habit of telling people who drive fast to slow down. He was driving extremely fast, either because he was showing off or just because he was made that way. I told him I felt fine about his driving. I even said I was enjoying it—despite the fact that I was rather attached to my life and wouldn't want to lose it in a road accident. With drivers like these you usually have nothing to fear. Mostly they just give occasional burst of speed to make themselves look big. Then they drive very tamely because basically they're scared. Mind you, there are people who really are obsessed with speed. Like James Dean—he was hooked on it.

'When did she die?'

'A few hours ago, in the Municipal Hospital. She's been unconscious for two days.'

I hadn't seen her for more than a year. The last time, I'd had a tape recorder with me and I'd asked her to sing me some songs in Rif dialect. She was a little embarrassed, but she smiled and began to sing. The words were about the joys of childhood, and gathering firewood, and harvest time, but her voice was sad. The worries of old age had taken a lot out of her. The fact that I was away so much meant that I missed her less. She must have been thinking, as she always did, about the distance between us. After all, I was the only clever one in the family. It was as if she were half dead and half alive. My feelings for her were awakened that morning. I had an emptiness in my soul. My health was in a pretty bad state. I only usually feel lonely on days when I'm sick.

Three in the morning. I wrestled with my hangover and forced myself to get up. I staggered across to the doorway and put a hairbrush in the crack so that it wouldn't shut. Another time I might not even have been capable of standing up. I was half awake and half asleep—I find I like being in that state because things you see in the clear light of day are never as beautiful as things that are half-dreamt. The dawn light was breaking. I hadn't seen dawn like this for years. The chassis of a crashed car, rusting near a tree. All that was left of the tree was a dried-out stump. The remains of a dead dog in the road, birds hovering overhead and more birds sitting on the electricity wires. I hadn't been to Sebta since Arhimo got married in Principe, more than ten years previously. It was the custom among my brother-in-law's tribe for the bride's eldest brother to carry her in his arms from the camel litter to the courtyard of the house. Abdelaziz found me drinking in a local bar with a number of old Spaniards, one of whom had lived in Tangier for a long time. He remembered the Jewish women from Eastern Europe coming to Tangier in the Nazi period, bringing with them small domestic birds in cages, and he remembered grilled sardines and onions in the wine shops, and wine from the barrel, and the boxes for seats, and how, every three glasses, it was drinks on the house, and how in those days there were always customers ready to volunteer a song.

At my sister's wedding I'd almost fallen while I was carrying her. The bride and groom broke the large round bread that had been baked for the wedding. The company scattered salt on the couple. They drank a bit of milk and ate dates. They put a big key in her hand. Women from the groom's family grabbed the embroidered handkerchiefs that decorated the camel litter, and also the pins that held the handkerchiefs on. This was supposed to neutralize the evil eye, or so they told me. The groom and his family had the upper hand. The bride's family were just looking on like servants. The groom made the shape of an arch with his arm at the doorway to the room, and the bride passed under his arched arm, bowing her head. I picked my way through the wedding guests to return to the bar with the middle-aged Spaniards.

'What did she die of?'

'A haemorrhage—a nose bleed. It didn't stop for a fortnight.'

The sound of a small bird crashing against the front of the car. Now it would no longer be able to pluck the berry it was dreaming of. A shepherd leading a small flock of sheep, followed by a skinny dog. A woman milking a cow. Chickens and their chicks. Sickly-looking children scratching up dirt with a stick. We overtook a man riding a broken-down bicycle and pedalling with difficulty. The bicycle was old. The daily grind was beginning. Morning was breaking in all its splendour. It looked glorious. I wrestled with my drowsiness. What I needed was a good cold beer. Malika had rung from Tetuan to ask if I could let her have 100 dirhams for dental work on a tooth that was keeping her awake at nights. That was when she'd told me about my father's death.

'When did he die?'

'Months ago.'

'Why didn't anyone tell me at the time he died?'

'Because we knew that you never got on with him.'

'But what are the neighbours going to think...?'

'They know that you two always hated each other...'

They did the same thing to me when my aunt died, as if I was no longer interested in who was alive and who was dead. They didn't tell me about anything except the weddings. It must have been my mother who had asked them to send for me. Even during the period when she'd fallen sick and was unconscious they hadn't told me.

The corpse of a donkey at the edge of a cornfield. The trees looked as if they were racing us and we were overtaking them. My brother-in-law's hands were steady on the steering wheel. He didn't smoke or drink. When I've had a bad night I usually find that my hand shakes with the first drink of the day. I lit a cigarette. The first drag made me dizzy. With the second drag I stuck my head out of the window to retch up air. My eyes were watering and I had a belly ache. He gave me a sideways glance. He'd never have let on openly that he disapproved of me.

My brother Abdelaziz told me:

'We made a nice grave for our father. You really ought to visit it some time.'

The graves of our brothers and sisters who had died during the years of famine had been wiped out, levelled by the wind and the rain. We're lucky nowadays because we're able to provide decent graves for our family when they die. This was what I told him and he was happy to hear me say it. Despite the crying of my sisters, Arhimo and Malika, and the weeping of two old women who had been my mother's friends in Tetuan, drowsiness got the better of me and I fell asleep. I woke up when the mourners' crying turned to wailing. The smell of rose water filled the laying-out room where they washed her body. The funeral procession started out towards the Sidi Mubarak cemetery. Death is a very final thing. Around me were twenty mourners whom I didn't know. In the street, others joined the procession. She didn't fit into the hole they'd made. They had to take her out again twice and one joker shouted:

'Hey, Abdullah, have respect for the woman! Stop tormenting her and dig her the grave she deserves!'

The gravedigger dug the edge of the grave a third time. I felt like chopping off his hands and gouging out his eyes. Even in death they wouldn't give her space in the earth. Rose water was sprinkled on the shroud. Then came the funeral prayer. Bread and figs were distributed to those present. There were no poor people there for the distribution of bread. Stuffed chicken with rice. An eagerness to eat, and a fierce argument between Arhimo and

Malika about the rights or wrongs of selling our house in Tetuan. Their husbands maintained a silent neutrality. We had built the house with the help of everyone in the neighbourhood, using stones from an earth-bank near where we lived. The women and the children, the unemployed, all of them had played a part in building this house. Our mother had always told us that we should only sell it if circumstances forced us to, and none of us was particularly needy at that point. I kept my own opinion to myself, but there seemed to be no way of breaking out of the argument. Eventually they gave up arguing and started to see about tea. I was overcome by a wave of dizziness which then gave way to nausea. I'd been smoking all day and my mouth was tasting vile. I was drinking only coffee. I pretended that I had to go out to buy cigarettes. Arhimo told me that I ought to cut down on the smoking and then she said:

'Abdelaziz will go out and buy you cigarettes if you can't do without them till tomorrow.'

I was dying to get out of the place. They noticed how itchy I was getting. My relations didn't say anything. My mother's funeral and selling our house, all on the same day. This had been the longest day of my life and I had never felt so bad. I knew that the death of my mother meant the death of my family. Arhimo was insistent that I returned straight away because she said that I didn't know the night in Sebta. She didn't realize that the night is my friend wherever I am. For me the night has always been a kind of escape route, whether in Barbès, the Barrio Chino in Barcelona, the Carmen area of Valencia, or Bab Marrakech in Casablanca. At that moment I wished I was in some place like a cave, with not even dripping water to disturb the silence. I don't remember how many bars I went into. After the second or third one everything became a confused blur. How had I left the city? I woke up to find myself in bed in my flat with all my clothes on. With the passing of the years I have tried in vain to remember how I got back to Tangier. One of my shoes was at the end of the bed, full of piss, and the other was on the bedside table, with wine dripping from it. I once knew a man who had pissed on his daughter while she was asleep in bed because he mistook the bed for the toilet. I hadn't pissed on anyone except myself. The day came when we sold the house and the money had to be apportioned according to Islamic law. My sisters began crying, silently, in the presence of the assessors, in this house of ours which we were now leaving for the last time. I asked our neighbour what was making them cry and he replied:

'Why do you think they're crying?! They're crying for the memory of your parents!'

I took 1,000 dirhams from my portion on the *taifor*, to match my brother's share, and I gave my sisters 1,000 dirhams each. They stopped their crying. I whispered to our neighbour:

'I tell you, this is all just a charade, and its characters are all clowns and hypocrites.'

I left Tetuan in the knowledge that the umbilical cord had been cut and that the roots of my family tree had now rotted beyond the point of no return.

28

A Love of Things That Could Not Be

This wasn't the first time that Saliya had come to Tangier from her small town. She'd come before as a visitor, but this time she'd decided to stay. Tangier, city of dreams; Tangier the naked, a boisterous city as transparent as crystal; Tangier the myth, the city that is all things to all people. Saliya didn't realize that Tangier crushes anyone who hasn't learned how to drink her enchanted wine. She is Circe the sorceress.[1] I know people who came here to write poetry and didn't even learn the language of the bars, and people who came to paint and didn't even know how to mix their colours.

This time when Saliya came, it was with a determination to stake everything in the hopes of winning the jackpot. This involved gambling her bottom half against her rough top half.

She was plunged into a wild life of drink and hashish. In the same way that mushrooms proliferate but don't grow, she had men quarrelling for her affections. Her kinds of mushrooms proved

---

1. The blonde sorceress Circe, queen of the island of Aeaea, was the daughter of Helios, god of the sun, and Perse, daughter of Oceanos, the god of the sea. She bewitched humans and animals with her magic potions. She changed Ulysses' friends into a herd of pigs, but Ulysses was saved from her spell because the god Hermes had armed him with a special herb that foiled the action of her potions.

poisonous for anyone who fell for her. She loved all men but wanted none. If she ever went with a man who found it difficult to get aroused, she would pretend that she was being raped, to excite him. She came from a good home, but she soon became like a curse on her family. From an early age she'd allowed her body to be raped by the teenagers of her town—and from other towns—and by the drunks and the hashish smokers. Her hand always trembled as she reached for her glass, and she could never be bothered to knock the ash off her cigarette. She once told her friend Carolina: 'Everyone who ever made me a promise always let me down.'

She soon gave up ideas of love and marriage, and learned how to get men to fight over her. She would write things in a notebook, in her terrible, shaky handwriting:

'You block my way at every point. What am I to do? There is no way out for me. You scare me, like some mythical monster. I am searching for a dream and I find no inspiration in you. You want me, but I want myself with that same strength with which you claim to want me.'

My friend Paloma also split her time between hashish, heavy drinking and writing down her thoughts.

'I really don't trust myself. And I write like a crazy person. If you ask me, I think that happiness is like a frog wearing a hat of peacock feathers. Love frightens me. I'm an angel with two black wings. A heart without an eye. I never wanted to travel to the edge of the abyss. Love doesn't matter to me any more; it's become like some dead whale, high and dry on a deserted beach in the heat of summer.'

In the midst of her heavy drinking and her nights of sex, something like remorse must have awakened in Saliya. She went back to live in the city she'd come from, in order to live in cleaner air and to regain her waking dreams. But then it was back to Tangier again, with her powders and cosmetics.

For three days the only food I had was the leftovers of customers at Mr Moh's café. The sea was rough, and the harbour area deserted, with no warships in, and no cargo ships either. This was in 1955. I was supposed to be getting the last remnants of a ship's crew back to their ship. They were drunk. There was an easterly wind blowing up a gale. I passed in front of the Bar María at about supper time. Abdeslam called me over. He offered me a glass of wine. I asked him for a loan of 5 pesetas to get something to eat. I understood from his protests that all he had was the price of a drink for himself and a drink or two for me. I thought: what do I do now? I ate the nuts that came with my drink. Then I also ate the nuts that came with his drink, and then the nuts of the man sitting next to him. He started ordering one drink after another, and he got so drunk that he was almost falling over. Babbling drunk. Before he left, I asked him for 1,000 pesetas and he gave it to me without batting an eyelid. I regretted not having asked him for more, because he'd surely have given it.

Saliya went to visit her teacher at his house because she wanted him to check through what she called one of her 'poetic texts'. They drank and smoked hashish together. Then, according to her version of events, when she refused to sleep with him, he tore her clothes and bit her on the neck and shoulder, leaving her with bite-marks. Saliya reckoned that on that particular night he was more drunk than she was, and she was more stoned than him. As it happened, he was going through an unsuccessful love affair with another girl student, whom he'd planned to marry, and Saliya had also been having a hard time because a boyfriend of hers had gone and married someone else.

Saliya came to Tangier at a time when even the best-looking prostitutes couldn't get work. If they were lucky they ended up marrying one of the unemployed. She found jobs as a cleaner in one of the hotels or in kitchens. All she had left was the glory of her defeated memories, a sad craziness, a frustration that came out in her drunkenness and the idle chatter of the bars.

Saliya would spend her nights in all kinds of places—in some luxury hotel somewhere or in a cheap dive—depending on her luck, or how drunk she was, or how well-off her client was. She didn't care who she went with. The night and her drunkenness hid the state she was in. She went from one house to another, until by the end she wasn't even charging for sex, but was just doing it to avoid confronting her craziness and restlessness. She'd be fucked by a different man every night, sometimes rich and sometimes poor, and sometimes by more than one, until morning came.

The daytime no longer meant anything for Saliya. Her nights had no day. Daytime made her ugly, while the night made her beautiful. The only thing that kept her going was the idea that one day, somehow, she might find someone to love. But love in Tangier is not the stuff of Platonic dreams. And in fact she ended up losing herself here and became just like all the others.

It was a period of poetry and a period of dreams in Tangier, but where were the poets and where were the dreamers? The truth was that defeat was walking the streets, in extremities of wretchedness and nakedness, walking wherever it wanted.

How did I meet Saliya?

I was alone in the lobby of the Hotel Villa de France when she came in. The waiter was talking to me about football and what he thought about the national squad and some of the local teams. When there were only one or two people in the lobby, he began cursing his fellow countrymen. Saliya ordered a beer and then lit a cigarette with a trembling hand. She opened a notebook, read a few lines and then placed it on the table. The waiter carried on with his conversation. She wrote and she drank. She lit one cigarette after another. She smoked them inhaling deeply. Only a little of the smoke came out from her mouth again, pale in colour, like a lizard in summer. She didn't seem to be one of 'them'. It was brave of her to drink beer if she wasn't a prostitute. She must have been a pretty liberated woman. I ordered a beer for her. She glanced at me and the waiter. She thanked me with a nod and a smile, and as we smoked and drank together I asked if it would be alright for me to sit with her. She agreed with a smile, lowering her head. The notebook was open. Her pen lay across the page, across what was written there. She didn't close the book when I sat next to her. I thought this was brave too. We asked each other's names. She said that she'd seen me with her teacher in her town the previous summer. He and I had been drinking in the kasbah and she'd been eating sardines with her friend Carolina. I took a furtive glance at the writing in her notebook.

'Who shall I go with today? I can't decide whether to go back or stay. There might be drinks for me tonight, but I won't go looking for them, and I won't be upset if there aren't any. Drink has a certain dignity.'

In my flat I had a strange sensation that her two nipples were peering at me. She emptied her glass each time I filled it. Then she wrote more thoughts in her notebook. Most of the time when she wrote she put the subject in the accusative and the object in the nominative. She wasn't too hot on grammar. I didn't have many books by the great poets, but I did have the ones who'd been killed by their love of poetry. She wasn't too keen on any of them. Her skin was white, but it was thick and taut and peppered with black spots. She had smiling eyes when she was relaxed, and long black eyelashes. These were probably the best thing about her. She had thin lips and her hair was curly. It smelt rather like a pile of autumn leaves that has been wetted for the first time by the rains. Sometimes when she hadn't bathed for a few days she smelt more like a goat. There was always a smell of drink and tobacco on her breath. We went to bed together. She kept her face to the wall. I woke up to find that she wasn't in bed, and when I went looking for her I found her asleep on the couch in the sitting room, cuddling a small pillow. I thought I should buy her a toy monkey or something. She was half asleep and half awake. She was the kind who chain-smoked. She'd get through one pack a night. In the morning I found the following written in her notebook:

'I dreamed that I crushed a butterfly and suddenly it turned into a bird and sprang up from under my feet. My father was chasing me in a garden and he fell into a well. My mother arrived. She was naked. She cried: 'Here's the grave!' Then she started dancing for joy. My father was calling for help, but my mother was going wild, rejoicing and dancing all over the place. My father's pathetic state in his old age drove her crazy because she was in love with another man.'

Saliya loathed the light of the morning in Tangier. Most of the time she wore black because it suited the whiteness of her skin. I never knew whether she realized how good it looked on her. She liked her nights in the streets and the noisy bars. A night of peace and quiet would have unsettled her. She spent her time fantasizing about men. She would take all kinds of risks with them, but in her case the risks didn't really matter. She was losing weight every day. Sometimes she gave herself to men who knew her, and sometimes to men who didn't. She would give sex without even charging for it, and in the morning all she would remember was the thumping of the bed, because more often than not the men who slept with her didn't even bother saying goodbye.

Saliya came to Tangier at the wrong time. In the Tangier night, her sex made her forget her head. She learned how to lie to herself and how to believe her lies. Nobody ever called her a liar because the people she mixed with were even bigger liars than she was. Liars are like drunks: they tend to stick together.

Saliya was betrayed by her youth and by her lack of experience of life. We drifted apart and I only saw her occasionally, in some bar or night club. Each of us went our separate ways. I was not the first or the last man in her life. I suppose that the strongest bond between us was a love of things that could not be.

Also by Mohamed Choukri
the first volume of his autobiography

FOR BREAD ALONE

Translated from the Arabic
with an Introduction by
Paul Bowles

A true document of human desperation, shattering in its impact. ***Tennessee Williams***

Mohamed Choukri's classic and moving work—which has already been translated into more than ten languages—speaks for an entire generation of North Africans.

Born in the Rif, Choukri moved with his family to Tangier at a time of great famine. His childhood was spent in abject poverty; eight of his brothers and sisters died of malnutrition or neglect. During his adolescence, described here with its attendant erotic escapades, Choukri worked for a time as servant to a French family. He then returned to Tangier, where he experienced the violence of the 1952 independence riots.

At the age of 20, and still illiterate, he took the decision to learn to read and write classical Arabic—a decision which transformed his life.

Saqi Books **ISBN 0 86356 138 1**